Kaddish

for a Child Not Born

Translated by

Christopher C. Wilson

and

Katharina M. Wilson

Northwestern University Press

Evanston, Illinois

Imre Kertész

Kaddish

for a Child Not Born

Hydra Books
Northwestern University Press
Evanston, Illinois 60208-4210

Originally published in Hungarian under the title *Kaddis a meg nem szvületett gyermekért* by Publ. Magvető, Budapest. Published 1997.

Printed in the United States of America

10 9 8 7 6 5 4 3 2

ISBN 0-8101-1176-4 (cloth)
ISBN 0-8101-1161-6 (paper)

Library of Congress
Cataloging-in-Publication Data

Kertész, Imre, 1929–
[Kaddis a meg nem született gyermekért. English]
Kaddish for a child not born / Imre Kertész ; translated by Christopher C. Wilson and Katharina M. Wilson.
p. cm.
ISBN 0-8101-1176-4 (cloth : alk. paper). — ISBN 0-8101-1161-6 (pbk. : alk. paper)
1. Holocaust survivors—Hungary—Fiction. I. Wilson, Christopher C. II. Wilson, Katharina M. III. Title.
PH3281.K3815K313 1997
894'.511334—dc21 97-3095
CIP

The paper used in this publication meets the minimum requirements of the American National Standard for Information Sciences—Permanence of Paper for Printed Library Materials, ANSI Z39.48-1992.

Cover: Börher, Hans. *Der Waldweg (Forest Path).* Courtesy of the Leopold Museum, Privatstiftung, Vienna.

"No," I said immediately and forthwith, without hesitation and spontaneously, so to say, for it is quite obvious that our instincts actually work against our instincts, so that, so to say, our anti-instincts act instead of, or even *as,* our instincts . . . So go my witticisms, if indeed these can be considered witticisms, that is, if naked, miserable truth can be considered a witticism. Thus I expound to the philosopher walking along with me after he and I both halted to catch our breath because of dieting, or sickness, or perhaps consumption in the midst of an almost audibly gasping oak forest, or glade, whatever you call it: I admit, I'm rather ignorant when it comes to trees; all I immediately recognize is the pine because of its needles, and the plantain because I like it, and what I like – even today – I recognize even by anti-instinct. I recognize it even if it is not by the same striking, stomach-gripping, ready to jump, in one word, inspired sort of recognition with which I recognize those things that I hate. I don't know why everything is always different with me than with others, or, rather, if I know why, it's simpler to know it in such a way that I don't. This way saves me the need for a lot of explanations. It does seem, though, that explanations are unavoidable; we are constantly explaining – that unexplainable complex of being and feeling and explaining ourselves; life itself demands explanations from us, as do our surroundings and finally as we do, demanding explanations from ourselves until, finally, we manage to minimize everything around us, ourselves included – that is to say, explaining ourselves to death. Thus I expound to the philosopher with that disgusting (to me) and yet irrepressible urge to speak, that which always seizes me when I have nothing to say, the urge, I suspect, which lies at the root of my habit of giving far too generous tips in restaurants, to cab drivers, to bribing official or semi-official representatives, and the like; it also might have something to do with my politeness, exaggerated to the point of self denial . . . as if I were continually apologizing for my existence, for this existence. Good God: I simply set out to take a walk in the forest – even if it is in this rather small oak forest – in the fresh air that is rather polluted – in order to clear out my head. Let's put it this way, because it sounds good as long as we don't look at the literal meaning of words, for if we do, then these words have no meaning whatsoever, for my head needs no *airing* out; on the contrary, I am extraordinarily sensitive to drafts. Here I spend – did spend – my time; temporarily (and this time I won't go into digressions suggested by the term) in the lap of Hungary's mountains, in a house, let's call it a resort, even though it would also do for a place of work. (I work all the time, not simply forced by necessity, but because if I didn't work I would have to exist, and if I existed, I don't know what I would be forced to do then, and it is better that I don't know, even though my cells and my genes probably suspect the answer, because that, precisely, is the reason why I keep working all the time; while I work, I am; if I didn't work, who knows if I'd be? So, I take this issue seriously. I have to take it seriously because, quite clearly, there is a very serious connection between my working and my existence.)

In sum, then, I'm staying at a place where I earned the right to be accommodated, in the distinguished company of my intellectual ilk whose company I cannot, therefore, avoid, regardless of how quietly I hide in my room – exposing the secret of my hiding place only by the pounding noise of my typewriter – and in spite of my tiptoeing along the corridor . . . after all, one has to eat – at which occasion my table companions surround me with their merciless presence. Also, one has to take an occasional walk, when, as now, I meet Dr. Oblath, the philosopher, in the midst of the forest, a man bursting with inappropriate vitality in his brown and beige checkered cap, wide-cut trenchcoat, narrow, light-colored eyes, and a face resembling soft dough, kneaded and already risen. Being a philosopher is his regular, worldly profession, which, incidentally, is confirmed by the appropriate entry on his personal papers, stating that Dr. Oblath is a philosopher just like Emmanuel Kant or Baruch Spinoza or Heraclitus of Ephesus. He is a philosopher in the same manner as I am a writer and literary translator, and the only reason why I don't place myself in that same ridiculous context among the giants lined up under the banner of my profession, those giants who once were *real* writers and, occasionally, *real* literary translators, is the fact that even without that analogical allegiance I'm ridiculous enough in my profession, and because in the eyes of some, translating is still a somewhat objectified activity, especially in the eyes of the authorities and even in my own eyes, albeit for different reasons, by way of the fact that it bestows some resemblance of an empirical craft upon my activities.

"No" something screamed and howled within me immediately and spontaneously when my wife (incidentally, she's no longer my wife) first mentioned it – you – and my panic-stricken cramp has only slowly, after many long years, been quieted down into some general melancholy Weltschmerz like Wotan's violent rage at the famous farewell, until slowly and maliciously, like incipient sickness, a question within me assumed definite shape from the fleeting shades of northern lights. This question is you, or more precisely I (and by and large Dr. Oblath was in agreement on that): *my existence in the context of your potentiality* or, in other words, I, as murderer, if with a bit of masochism we take the question's logic to a *reductio ad absurdum*. This reduction is quite permissible for, thank God, it's too late, it will always be too late; you don't exist and I am in full cognizance of myself, since with this "no" I destroyed everything, demolished everything, above all, my ill-fated short-lived marriage . . . so I told Dr. Oblath, professor of philosophy, with an indifference which life didn't manage to teach me but which I practice quite expertly now whenever it's essential. And right now it was essential because the philosopher was nearing me in a pondering mood; I could see it in the slightly inclined pose of his head, on which his rascally visored cap perched; he approached like a humorous highwayman with a few drinks already down his gullet, pondering whether to knock me down or content himself with the loot. But of course – I almost said, alas – Oblath wasn't pondering that; philosophers don't usually ponder highwaymen unless in the form of some deep philosophic inquiry, and the dirty work is always done by professionals; after all, we have seen that. However, it was mere whim, not suspicion, that prompts this association with Dr. Oblath, for I know nothing of his past and hopefully he won't tell me about it. He didn't, but he surprised me with a no less indiscreet question – like a highwayman asking how much money I had in my pockets – for he inquired about my family circumstances. Admittedly, he prefaced his question by informing me of *his* situation, as if by giving me an advance, so to say, postulating that by my finding out everything about him – even though I was not in the least interested – he acquired the right to know about my . . . but I stop this string of reflections because I feel the letters, words sweeping me, sweeping me away in the wrong direction, the direction of moralizing paranoia in which I often find myself nowadays and whose reasons are painfully obvious (loneliness, solitariness, self-imposed exile). It's not that these reasons worry me – after all, they are all my own doing, each like a dig with the spade in the process of digging, dirtful by dirtful, that deep ditch which I have to dig consistently and eternally so that it may be, and which will swallow me up (albeit it might happen that I'll dig in air rather than in dust since it's more spacious) – at any rate, all Dr. Oblath did was to ask the innocent question of whether or not I had a child: admittedly, though, he asked it with the rude honesty characteristic of philosophers, that is to say, inconsiderately and at the worst possible moment. But then, again, I can't deny this; how was he to know that his question would upset me? Still, owing to my exaggerated politeness, exaggerated to the point of self-denial, I replied to his question with an uncontrollable urge to speak, which while it flowed never ceased to disgust me; so in spite of all, I told him.

"No," I said immediately and forthwith, without hesitation and spontaneously, so to say, for it is quite obvious that our instincts actually work against our instincts and that, so to say, our anti-instincts act instead of, or even *as,* our instincts. Yes, for all the idiotic speeches for my self-imposed and totally unjustifiable (although I have plenty of reasons, some of which I mentioned earlier, I believe) minimization of myself, I wanted to make up to Mr. Oblath, Ph.D., or Dr. Oblath, professor of philosophy, when I described him in the midst of the oak forest (or was it maple?) the way I did, although I still maintain the verity of the details: the visored cap, the wide coat as well as the acidy narrow eyes, and the face resembling kneaded and risen dough. All I'm saying is that all the above could have been stated differently in a more balanced, more generous, I almost said more affectionate way. But I'm afraid. I can do no differently; I am only able to depict in this manner, with my pen dipped in sarcasm, derisively, perhaps even humorously (although that's not up to me to judge), but also to a certain degree lamely, as if someone continued to push back my pen constantly whenever it tried to form certain words, so that, in the end, my hand substitutes other words, words that never manage to depict an affectionate portrait – simply because, I'm afraid, it's possible that there is no love *in me,* but – good God – whom on earth could I love? And why? After all, Dr. Oblath spoke cordially, so much so that I even noted down some of his more poignant observations because they struck my fancy. He, too, is childless, he said, he has no one except an aging wife, caught in fighting the problems of aging – or so I understood, for the philosopher expressed himself less concretely, more discreetly, so to say, leaving it to me to understand what I wanted to understand and even though I didn't, I still did. Anyway, Dr. Oblath continued, the subject of his childlessness only occurred to him in the recent past, but then, quite frequently, as even now, he was pondering it walking the forest path and, you see, he couldn't resist raising the subject. It's on his mind presumably because he, too, is getting on in years and consequently some possibilities, such as the potential of having a child, gradually dissipate for him, become impossibilities, and that it is actually only nowadays, and nowadays very frequently, that he ponders this, and as he put it, he ponders it as "a loss," something "he missed out on." At this point Dr. Oblath stopped (for in the meantime we started walking down the path, two kindred souls, two men engaged in conversation, two sad spots on the canvas of the landscape painter, two soil spots fundamentally disturbing nature's probably never really existing harmony – only I can't recall whether I joined Oblath or he me, but we won't make a capital case of this, oh, a question of vanity – yes, naturally, I joined Dr. Oblath, probably in order to allow myself to get rid of him, because this way I could turn around anytime I chose); here, then, Dr. Oblath stopped and strained his risen, here and there almost overflowing doughy face by way of throwing back his head with its rascally cap and fixing his gaze on a tree limb across the path; the gaze hung there like a miserable, worn-to-shreds piece of clothing, ready to serve even in its abandonment. And while we stood there, in silence, I in Oblath's, Oblath in the tree's force field of gravity, I had the feeling that I was about to be witness to a presumably confidential revelation by the philosopher. And so it happened. When Dr. Oblath finally spoke, he said that by saying that he feels a loss, because of what happened, or rather because of what didn't happen, he wasn't thinking of the concept of continuity, this rather abstract, yet, let's admit it, fundamentally satisfying reassurance, derived from knowing that one has (or, rather, has not) fulfilled one's personal and suprapersonal responsibility on earth that is beyond the continuation of existence, his contrived survival in the generations of his offspring, his immortality which beyond mere continuation is man's so-called transcendental – although also very practical – obligation vis-à-vis life, preventing him from feeling truncated, superfluous, and, in the final analysis, impotent. He is not thinking of the frightening prospect of lonely, supportless old age, he said, no, he is in truth afraid of something else, of "emotional atrophying," said Dr. Oblath, precisely in those terms, as he started down the path anew toward the resort building, supposedly, but in fact now I realize, toward emotional atrophying. And on this path I faithfully resolved to accompany him, appropriately moved by his moving words, though less taken by his fear, which, I'm afraid (or rather, I hope, nay, I am convinced, I know) is only a momentary fear and in that sense sacred and only a fear that can be submerged in eternity as if in a bowl of consecrated water, for when it materializes, we won't fear it anymore, we won't even remember what it was we had feared because it will have taken over our being, we will be totally submerged in it, it will be ours and we will be its. This, too, is simply digging the ditch, digging the ditch for the grave I am digging in the air (because I'll be comfortable being there) and, therefore, I say – not to the philosopher, only to myself – one need not be afraid of emotional atrophying; one must accept it or even welcome it, like a helpful hand that, although undoubtedly it is helping us toward the grave, still helps us along – "this world is not directed against us, and even though it has its pitfalls we have to try to love them"; even though I interject, addressing not the philosopher, not even this hack who was able to receive all those letters from Rainer Maria Rilke. I say this only to myself, *I love only these pitfalls,* and I think to myself, this, too, can't be entirely right; here, too, there is a false note, one that I keep hearing just like some conductors immediately recognize when, let's say, the English horn, due to a misprint in the score, blows a note too high. And I hear this false note not only within but also without in my immediate as well as larger surroundings, even in my cosmic environment, so to say, and I hear it continuously, as I do here, in the lap of decaying nature, the sick oaks (or are they maples?), the stinking brush, and in the dirty sky shimmering through the consumptive branches, here, where I don't in the least feel the inspiration of the thought "to be a creator, to engender, to create a form," which idea, don't you agree, would be totally useless without its constant validation and manifestation in the world; it would cease to exist without the multifarious harmony of consent by all the animate and inanimate objects of the world . . . Yes, for in spite of the fact that our depression (to leave the rest unsaid) is secret, if we listen, quietly, to the racing of our blood and to our nightmares, in secret – and this is the only context where I do feel the multifarious harmony of everything and everyone – we know that, still, we do want to live, more than anything, we want to live, thus lethargically, thus joylessly, thus ill, yes, even if and even when we can't, one cannot live . . . For that reason and partially also to avoid getting stuck in this sentimental mood in which, as everywhere or at least everywhere *I* participate, I clearly hear the false note of the English horn again, so, for this reason I asked him some very appropriately professional, philosophic – but probably not in the least wise – questions: "Why is it like this? All this mass? Where and when did we pawn off our rights? Why can't we ultimately and finally not know what we know?" etc., etc., as if I didn't know what I know, driven by my undefeatable urge to speak as by the pangs of some terrible horror. And in consequence on Dr. Oblath's face there settled a professionally philosophic, professionally Hungarian mid-mountain, middle-class, middle-of-the-road, middle-age, mid-stature expression reflecting the middle-of-the-road views of a middle-rank academic.

The wrinkles of his cynical, happy smile completely swallowed up his narrow eyes. Immediately, too, an objectivity, even detachment, returned to his voice characterized by sanctimoniousness, and in general he became quite self-confident again, a man whose confidence was only momentarily shaken by the threatening proximity of something real and flesh and blood a little earlier; thus we walked slowly homeward: two actually well-dressed, well-fed, and well-preserved, middle-aged middle-rank academics espousing middle-of-the-road views, two survivors (each in his own way), two still living, two half-dead men. We talked the way two academics can talk, totally superfluously. We discussed – peaceful and bored – why one can't be; that the mere existence of life is simply a phenomenon of ignorance because considering it more profoundly, from a privileged point of view, one should not be allowed to live; we only put up with it because of past occurrences and the reoccurrence of past events; not to mention the fact that more advanced concepts have long prohibited the existence of life. The subject also came up – but of course I don't remember everything since this chance conversation borne of mere confusion and embarrassment carried or, rather, was confused by hundreds and hundreds of similar conversations from the past, just as a single creative idea is filled with the grandeur and magnificence of a thousand nights of lovemaking born anew from oblivion every time. Thus, I can't recall everything, but I think the subject arose as to whether or not it might be possible that the unconscious efforts of existence directed to being might not be the manifestations of some naïveté – which now would be quite impossible – but that, contrarily, a sign of the fact that it can only continue this way, without knowing, if, indeed, it needs to continue. And if in the final analysis survival isn't achieved, which of course can only be achieved at a higher level (Dr. Oblath), then (we both together) there are not only not the slightest indicators for this idea but its opposite appears to be the case, namely the collapse into ignorance ... Further, that intentional ignorance is obviously the symptom of schizophrenia ... And further, that, accordingly, in order to cope with the state of the world today (me) and its realization (Dr. Oblath), for which efforts are extended, incidentally, by all worlds everywhere, without the assistance of faith, culture, and other ceremony, only catastrophes ... And so on, and so on we blew the false notes of the English horn as the thin, bluish dusk descended on the motionless, frozen tops of the trees of the glade in whose depth like unto a thick center hid the dense mass of the resort building where dinner awaited us, with tables set and the expectation of the sounds of silver and china, glasses clinking, and the chattering sound of conversation, and from this, too, the false notes of the English horn emanated, just as I couldn't deceive myself about the fact that, after all, I didn't turn around in order to escape Dr. Oblath, that I remained at his side to the very end, hypnotized, and on account of my emptiness covered by this urge to speak, this emptiness because of which I had a bad conscience. I stayed with him so that I wouldn't see, wouldn't have to talk of the subject of which I would have to speak, or who knows, perhaps even write. Yes, indeed: and the night punished me – or was it a reward? – for all this by bestowing a large, sudden thunderstorm, crackling thunder, forbodingly illuminating strokes of lightning, long, zigzagged hieroglyphs first spanning across the whole sky, then dissipating and the dry, short, and clearly – or at least clearly to me – legible letters that read:

"No!" something screamed, howled within me, immediately and forthwith, and it was only gradually, after many, many years had quieted it down, that my cramp gave way to a quiet but persistent pain, until slowly and maliciously, like a malignant sickness, a question began to take distinct shape within me: "Were you to be a dark-eyed little girl? With pale spots of scattered freckles around your little nose? Or a stubborn boy? With cheerful, hard eyes like blue-gray pebbles?" Yes, my existence in the context of your potentiality. And that whole night I pondered nothing but that question, be it in the blinding illumination of lightning or with sparking eyes in the dark, where, in the capricious intervals of the atmospheric rage, I saw the question dancing on the walls, so to say, so that I have to consider these sentences which I'm now writing down on paper as if they had been written at night, even though that night I lived rather than wrote. I lived on, or rather, I was beset by a slew of pains, mostly of the reminiscent type. (I also had half a bottle of cognac.) It's possible I only put down a few confused words onto the pages of my eternally present notebook or writing pad, words I couldn't reconstruct later on and if I did then I didn't understand them. I forgot everything, and it was only years later that the night came to life again within me, and many years had to pass again until, as now, I was able to try and write down what I was going to write that night had I been writing that night, if, anyway, a single night were not too short for writing down what I would have written.

But how could I have written it down then when that night was only the beginning, perhaps not the very first but in any case one of the initial steps toward clairvoyance. That is to say, toward the long, long – who knows how long? – road of self-liquidation, the initial shovel digs for the grave I am digging for myself – now

I no longer have doubts – it's in the clouds where I make my bed. And this question – my life in the context of the potentiality of your existence – proved to be a good guide. Yes, as if you led me, nay, dragged me, by your fragile little hand on this path which in the final analysis leads nowhere, or, at best, to a totally unseen, totally unalterable self-recognition, and on which path one set forth by removing the obstacles, the protruding obstacles in the way. Did I say "can" – for here not even "must" is meaningful. First, and foremost, I must proceed by the elimination, I would even say total eradication, of my mid-intellectual status, even if I only do this as really simply a precautionary measure, as if I were, or rather, had been, a cautious, promiscuous person moving in AIDS-affiliated circles, for I no longer belong to the mid-intellectual class, I'm not even an intellectual, I am nothing; I was born a private man, said J.W.G. . . . I remain a private survivor, say I; at most I am (since I exist and must be something) a literary translator to a certain extent. That's the reason why, finally, I have even foregone the pitiful existence of a successful Hungarian author in spite of threatening circumstances; I did so even though my wife (she has been someone else's wife for a long time) told me: "You have every talent" (she scared me a lot by that). She said she is not suggesting that I give up my artistic or any other ideas, but that I stop having little faith, and that the less I compromise my artistic or other ideas, the more I have to try to realize these ideas, and thus myself, which means that I should aim to be successful, she said, for that is everyone's ambition, even that of the world's greatest writers, she said. "Don't kid yourself," my wife said, "if you don't want to be successful, then why do you bother to write at all?" She asked this undoubtedly tough question, but then that question's time hadn't come yet; the sad thing is that she was probably entirely right, she probably saw straight into my entrails; I probably have – had – all the talent for the pitiful existence of a successful Hungarian writer whose transparent ins and outs I knew so well and pursuing which I have – I had – the necessary talents: if not, I know – I would have known – how to acquire them by sublimating my total sense of insecurity and fear of existence into a simple, blind, uninhibited, nervous, not necessarily fascinating but at least somewhat spectacular self-adoration, if I transformed it into moralizing paranoia and the uninterrupted process of accusing others. However, and this is even more dangerous, it is even more likely that I had the talent for the equally miserable existence of an unsuccessful Hungarian writer, and here, again, I must give credit to my wife who, again, was right in this regard, for if one takes the path of success, then one ends up either successful or unsuccessful, *there is no third* alternative; and, for sure, both paths are equally miserable, which is the reason why I escaped – in lieu of alcoholism – into the objective delusion of literary translating for a while. In this manner, as I remembered my wife's words, I remembered my wife too, whom I have long ceased to remember; in fact, I don't even remember her when, very infrequently, intentionally or unintentionally, we meet somewhere; it probably is intentionally and almost invariably at the initiative of my (ex) wife, who, come to think of it, must feel some remote, totally unwarranted sense of guilt mixed with nostalgia toward me. I recognize this – to the extent I do – I always guess that the nostalgia she might feel (if she does) is probably attributable to her youth and to the few short years she wasted on me, and the totally unwarranted sense of guilt, in turn, is perhaps occasioned by the fact that she has been unquestionably right, but that her right was also never questioned, and as such her sense of right was acquired without any of the usual resistance – in other words, that I never accused her of anything; but – good God! – what on earth could I accuse her of or could I ever have accused her of? Accuse her, perhaps, of wanting to live?

In this manner, thus, as I remembered her words, I remembered her, I remembered my ill-fated and short-lived marriage, I remembered and saw it in front of my eyes, laid out as if on a dissection table. And if I observe the cooled corpse of my marriage tenderly, lovingly, yet with detachment, the way, in the final analysis, in which I view everything, then I have to be careful not to construct some cheap, dirty little victories out of my wife's above-mentioned words, which, undoubtedly, did their best to annoy me. On this lightning-illuminated night, though, when I feel myself at such a distance from my marriage and when I lack understanding to such a degree that my total lack of understanding finally resolves everything as entirely simple and understandable – on this all-illuminating night, I must know that it was *the drive to live* that made my wife utter these words; it was her drive to live that needed my success to alleviate the momentous ill luck that became her inheritance as a result of her birth; that hated, incomprehensible, unacceptable ill luck she bore not as ill luck but, contrarily, as a glorious halo, so to say – no, that's an exaggeration, let's say she bore it like a translucent fragile shell, which at the moment of our first encounter I myself had noticed quite spontaneously as she – somewhere, in someone's apartment, at some so-called party – suddenly separated herself from the mass of chatterers, that ancient, formless, and yet related mass of live flesh, expanding, moving in waves, and contracting in cramps; she departed from there and passed over a blue-green carpet as if over the sea, leaving behind her the cut-open body of a dolphin, and she walked victoriously yet shyly toward me, and I thought immediately and spontaneously to myself: "What a beautiful Jewess!" – and I still do it, even nowadays, when, very infrequently and almost invariably on my (ex) wife's initiative, we meet somewhere and I look at her head bent forward, the avalanche of her shiny thick hair framing her face as she is writing one prescription after another on the small table in the café for me: sleeping pills, relaxants, happy pills, crazy pills, so that I will bear it as long as I have to, and since I have to bear it, at least I should see, hear, and feel what I have to see, hear, and feel all doped up. I haven't said this yet, but why should I have since I know it anyway ... so why do I act as if these notes were relevant to anyone but me, although, of course, they are relevant; I write because I have to write, and whenever one writes *one sustains a dialogue,* I read somewhere; while God still existed one sustained a dialogue with God, and now that He no longer exists one has to sustain a dialogue with other people, I guess, or, better still, with oneself, that is to say, one talks or mumbles to oneself. Anyway, I hadn't said yet that my wife (she has been someone else's wife for a long time) is a doctor. No, she is not a specialist in some serious illness – that I couldn't have put up with, not even temporarily – no, she is only a dermatologist, although she does take it seriously, just like anything else. Yes, as she is writing my prescriptions (because this is how I – cunningly and subversively – take advantage and subvert our occasional and totally innocent rendezvous) I still sometimes think: "What a beautiful Jewess!" Okay, but how different those thoughts are now, how discouraged, tame, pitiful, pitying myself, her, everyone, and everything, miserable, not at all like then, when I thought "What a beautiful Jewess!" Yes, that way naturally, and shamelessly, electrifying my male flesh, the way some male specimen would think, a macho, a stud, like the rest of that shameless fraternity who always think this way: what a beautiful Jewess; what a beautiful gypsy girl; what a fine Negress; French women; women with glasses, my boy; big-breasted women; big-butted women; small-breasted but big-butted women, etc., etc. However, in case I didn't know it, I was enlightened as to the fact that this way of thinking was by no means limited to male studs, no, not in the least! Female studs think precisely the same way or, rather, precisely the same way only invertedly, which in the final analysis is the same. I learned this some time ago in an aquarium-lit café where I was waiting for my ex-wife. Two women, two beautiful young women were conversing at the next table when suddenly the world turned around, but almost literally, with a sudden, wrenching sense of vertigo it turned me back, threw me back to my faraway childhood and to an ancient trauma of mine whose origin – how shall I put it – was a shocking, startling spectacle, one commanding a lifelong shock. With which spectacle, who knows why (for who could know a soul's transparent secrets, and if one knew, why wouldn't one try to escape them since they are not only offensive but also boring), with which spectacle, then, I later identified myself, so much so that even if it didn't happen in full reality (to use this meaningless phrase) I still felt that I was turning into this spectacle, that I *am* that spectacle, the spectacle I saw in a dusty, stuffy Hungarian village where I was sent for a summer vacation. Yes, there it was that I lived among Jews for the first time, real genuine Jews, I mean, not Jews like we were – city Jews, Budapest Jews, that is to say, not Jews at all, but of course not Christians either; we were the kind of non-Jewish Jews who still observe holy days, long fasts, or at least, definitely, until lunch. No, indeed, the village relatives (I no longer remember how we were related, why should I, anyway, they have dug their graves a long, long time ago in the air where the smoke from their remains dissipated), *they* were real Jews: prayer in the morning, prayer in the evening, prayer before food, prayer with the wine . . . other than that, they were fine people, though unbearably boring, of course, for a little boy from Budapest. I believe the war had already started then, but as everything was still quiet and beautiful here, we merely practiced darkening the windows; Hungary was the island of peace in a Europe that exploded in flames; *here it couldn't happen,* what happened and is continually happening in, let's say, Germany or Poland or the "Czech protectorate" or France or Serbia or Slovakia, in other words, everywhere else all around us. No, not here. How could it? Yes, one morning at my relatives' I opened the bedroom door unawares and then immediately turned back screaming, not aloud, though, only within me, because I saw somebody monstrous, something awful that struck me as obscene and for which – if only on account of my age – I was not prepared: *I saw a bald woman in a red gown in front of a mirror*. And it took a while until my confused and terrified head would identify that woman with my aunt, whom on other occasions (even after the *event*) I was accustomed to seeing with a strangely stiff and thin but otherwise normal head of reddish brown hair. I didn't dare to make a squeak, much less ask questions; with all my heart I hoped that she didn't notice my watching. I lived in the thick, dark air of secrets and disgust; my relative's denuded, shining head, resembling a mannequin in a display window, evoked the image of a corpse or of a great harlot into which she metamorphosed at night. Only much later and, of course, only at home did I dare raise the question as to whether I actually saw what I saw, for even *I* began to wonder whether or not it really happened. My father's laughing face did not put me at rest, not at all, for I felt his laugh was frivolous, yes, frivolous and destructive, even if only self-destructive, although these words were not part of my vocabulary – after all, I was still a child. I simply found his laughter to be idiotic because he did not comprehend my great horror, disgust, my life's first great, spectacular metamorphosis. No, he didn't in the least comprehend the horror of seeing a *bald woman sitting in front of a mirror* in the place of the familiar relative. Instead of alleviating my pain, he topped it with additional horror – admittedly good-humoredly – as he explained (from which explanation I understood nothing except for the sheer horror of the facts or, rather, the pure, mysterious, incomprehensible factuality of the facts as he explained) that our relatives are Polians, and that Polian women shave their heads for religious reasons and wear wigs. Later on, when my Jewishness gradually began to assume more importance, that is to say, when the news began to spread that that condition usually carries the death penalty, probably simply so I could grasp this incomprehensible and strange fact – that is, my being a Jew – in its appropriately strange yet at least more familiar light, then I suddenly found myself understanding who I was: *a bald woman in a red gown in front of a mirror*. This was a clear thing, even if it wasn't pleasant, and most of all incomprehensible, yet in the final analysis my recognition gave definition to my unpleasant and rare incomprehensible situation, explained, I'd almost say, where I belonged. Then, finally it turned out that I no longer needed this because I finally made my peace with this idea, my Jewishness, that is, as I did with all the other unpleasant, and, above all, not very comprehensible ideas. I made my peace with them slowly, gradually, one after the other; only a cease-fire, mind you, knowing that these unpleasant and, above all, not very understandable ideas will also cease when I cease to be, and until then these ideas are quite useful. Especially useful among them is the idea of my Jewishness, of course, only as an unpleasant and, above all, not very understandable state of facts, a state that is occasionally lethal but for me (and I hope, I even trust, that not everyone agrees with me on this account; I believe there will be those who will resent me, and moreover I sincerely hope that some will outright hate me for it, especially the Jewish and non-Jewish Semites and anti-Semites) – as I say, for me its usefulness is contained precisely in this: I can only and exclusively use it this way and no other – as an unpleasant and, above all, not very understandable, additionally occasionally lethal state of facts which *we must try to love* as we can for its danger only. Although, as far as I am concerned, I see no reason for it, perhaps because I have long ceased to try to live in harmony with people or with nature or even with myself; moreover, I'd see some sort of outright moral depravity in this same disgusting perversity as in an Oedipal relationship or some blood contagion between siblings. Yes, there I sat and waited for my (ex) wife in that aquarium-lit café, expecting oodles of new prescriptions and not even thinking about my unpleasant and, above all, not very understandable and additionally occasionally lethal existence, while two women at the next table conversed and I began, automatically, so to say, to eavesdrop because they were beautiful women; one blondish, the other brownish, and still, regardless of how much and how often they have disappointed me in the past (just to mention this in passing), secretly, when quietly and carefully I listen to my blood and my nightmares, secretly I love beautiful women even thus: with some sort of unshakable, unceasing, I could even say natural attraction which, precisely because it wants to appear banally obvious, is, in fact, mysterious because it exists almost totally independent of me and as such it's even annoying and cannot be dismissed with the same ease as, for example, my love of plantains, which I love, quite simply, because of their massive, spotted trunks, magnificent and fantastic limbs, and the huge, veined leaves hanging in the appropriate season like tired dangling hands. And as I entered their conversation, albeit as a passive participant, a conversation whose confidential, one could almost say muffled tone immediately promised an important subject matter, I heard these words right away: "I don't know, I couldn't with a stranger . . . I couldn't with a black man, or a gypsy, an Arab . . . " Here the voice ceased but I felt a sense of hesitation, my sense of rhythm told me that this sentence is not finished, that something had to follow, and I almost started to fidget in my seat because I knew quite well, naturally, what was bound to follow, I was about to whisper it to her when, finally, she added: " . . . or with a Jew." And then all of a sudden, but totally unexpectedly, since I anticipated the word, lay in waiting for it, almost demanded it from them, all of a sudden, still, the world turned topsy-turvy with a sudden, stomach-gripping sense of vertigo; I thought, if that woman looks at me now I'll metamorphose: I'll be a *bald woman in a red gown in front of a mirror*. There is no escaping this curse, I thought, none whatsoever. I thought I saw only one way out: to get up from my table right away and either beat up or fuck that woman. Needless to say, I did neither, just as I didn't do so many times and so many things that I thought – often for good reason – I ought to do. And this didn't even belong to those categorical imperatives, breaking which I would have had to justifiably shake my head in disgust. The urge to act barely rose up when it extinguished itself as a few disparate but familiar thoughts came my way: why convince this woman or even myself, for I am convinced of everything, and have been for a long time. I do what I have to do, although I don't know why I have to. I still do it in the hope, nay, in the firm conviction, that someday there will be no compulsion and I'll be allowed to stretch myself on my comfortable place of rest, after, of course, I have been thoroughly worked to the bone and made to jump through the hoops in order to dig my grave and at present – even though so much time has passed – Good Lord – I'm still only in the process of digging.

Then my wife arrived too, and I thought, with unleashed emotions, forthwith and spontaneously, so to say: "What a beautiful Jewess!" as she walked across the bluish-green carpet as if across the ocean and headed victoriously yet still shyly directly toward me, because she wanted to talk to me for she found out who I was. B., author and literary translator, one of whose works she had read concerning which she just had to talk with me. Thus spoke my once and future (future then, once now) wife. She was very young then, ten years younger than I, actually back then I wasn't that old either, but old enough – then as always. Yes, that is the way I see her even now, at night, every stormy lightning-illuminated night, and also in my later, much later, nights of darkness. Yes, *I wonder why I spent my lonely nights dreaming of the song . . . and I am again with you . . .* I whistled, amazed that I whistled, amazed even more that I whistled a stardust melody we used to whistle all the time; nowadays I only whistle Gustav Mahler, exclusively Gustav Mahler, Symphony no. 9. But this, I feel, is irrelevant. Unless, of course, someone happens to know Mahler's Symphony no. 9, judging by whose tenor he could rightly and with good reason assess my state of mind, that is, if he is interested and does not content himself with indirect references uttered by me from which the necessary inferences can similarly be extracted. *When our love was new and each kiss a revelation.*

"No!" something howled, screamed from within me; I don't want to remember, in this respect, not even in the sense of the famous *...* dipping ladyfingers into premixed spiced tea instead of the famous *...*. Although, of course, I do want to remember, I do, I don't, I can't help it; if I write, I remember, I have to remember, even though I don't know why I have to, probably because of knowledge; memory is knowledge we live in order to remember what we know because we must not forget what we know; don't worry, children, I'm not talking of some "moral obligation," no, please, all I'm saying is that we are unable, we *cannot* forget, this is the way we were created; we live in order to know and remember, however, perhaps, or probably, or even quite certainly, we know and remember in order to make sure that some will be ashamed because of us. Yes, we remember for those who are or aren't – it's all the same – because they either are or aren't; what's important is that we remember, know and remember so that someone – anyone – can be ashamed because of us and (perhaps) for us. For, as far as I'm concerned, if I got started on my privileged, extraordinary – I almost said consecrated (well, I don't mind using big words, consecrated it is, consecrated in the black mass of humanity), yes, on my consecrated memories, dripping gas and shaken by harsh voices: *Der springt noch auf*; for them the last *soma Jiszroel* of the Warsaw fugitive would *howl* and then the explosion of the collapse of the world . . . And then, very quietly, and every day anew a surprising awareness about to be hidden would come over me: well, well, I did get up, *ich sprang doch auf*, yes, even more, I am still here, although I don't know why; accidentally, I guess, as I was born; I am as much or as little an accomplice to my staying alive as I was to my birth. All right, I admit, there is a tiny bit more shame in staying alive, especially if one does everything within one's power—but that's all, no more. I was not willing to give in, like an idiot, to the mass survival hysteria and the breast-pounding oratory, Good God! *Man is always a little at fault*, that's all. I stayed alive, therefore I am, I thought . . . no, I didn't think anything, I simply existed like a Warsaw fugitive, like a Budapest survivor, one who makes no fuss over his survival, who does not feel compelled to testify to his survival, to give meaning to it – yes – to turn his survival into a triumph however quiet, however discreet and personal, but still, essentially, the only genuine, the only possible triumph through which the survivor – that is, I myself – makes the prolonged and multiple survival of himself possible in descendants – you . . . No, I didn't think about it, didn't think that I was supposed to think of it until the night descended upon me, that all-illuminating and yet totally dark night, and the question was put before me (actually, behind me, behind my life, since, thank heavens, it's late, and now it will always be too late), the question, yes, of whether you would be a dark-eyed little girl? With faint dots of scattered freckles around your little nose? Or a stubborn boy with gay and hard eyes like silver-blue gravel? Yes, my life in the context of your potentiality, or anyhow, examined in any context, strictly, sadly, without anger or hope, just as one looks at an object. As I said, I wasn't thinking of anything, even though I should have. Because secretly there was some mole-work going on, digging and undermining, something I should have been aware of and of course I did know about, I only believed it to be something other than what it was. What was it? I don't know, but I suspect that I took it for some encouraging activity, just as that blind old man mistakes the ringing, clinging noise of spades for work on the sewer, even though they are digging a grave – in fact, his own. At any rate, I found myself writing because I had to write, although I didn't know why. The fact is I found myself working with unceasing, I'd say mad, diligence. I always work, and I'm not only forced to do so to support myself, but if I didn't work I would live, and if I lived then I don't know what I'd be forced to do; it's better that I don't know, although my cells, my intestines certainly suspect why . . . that's why I work and work unceasingly; while I work I am, if I didn't work, who knows whether or not I'd be? Therefore, I have to take all this seriously because there are very serious connections between my survival and my work; this is a totally obvious and not in the least normal thing, even though there are others, and quite a few of them, who also write because they have to, although not everyone who writes has to write. For me, this is a fact, writing is necessity, I don't know why, but it seems this was the only solution offered to me, even if it doesn't solve anything; still, it doesn't leave me, how shall I say it, in the state of insolubility which I would be forced to consider insoluble even in its insolubility and could, therefore, be tortured aside from the state of insolubility of the frustration over it. Looking back now, I think it's possible I used writing as an escape (and not entirely without reason, albeit I believed myself to be escaping in a different direction, toward a different goal, than in actuality I was escaping and keep on escaping even now), I believed it to be an escape, even salvation; my own salvation and that of my physical or, to use fancy words, that of my spiritual world. I believed it to be absolutely essential for demonstrating that world for him – anyone – who will be ashamed because of us and (perhaps) for us. This night was inevitable; it had to happen so that I may finally learn to see in the darkness, to see, among other things, the nature of my work which in the final analysis is nothing but digging, the continued digging of that grave which others had started digging for me in the air, others who hastily, simply because they didn't have the time to finish, and not even with some sort of devilish mockery, oh no, simply, uncaringly, not even looking around, put the tool in my hand and left me to finish myself what I now know to be their work. Thus, every recognition of my life was merely a recognition leading up to this one, and whatever I did turned into a recognition leading up to this one, my marriage as much as my work.

"No," I said forthwith and immediately, without hesitation and spontaneously, so to say, yes, still spontaneously, for the time being, anyway, even if by instinct working against my natural instincts, my nature even. Thus this "no" was not a decision, not a free decision in the sense of choosing between "yes" or "no";

no, this "no" was a recognition, a decision not made or makable by me but a decision made concerning me. It wasn't even a decision: it was the recognition of my sentencing, and it was only a decision in the limited sense of not deciding against the decision, which, undoubtedly, would have been the wrong decision, for how can one decide against one's fate, to use that grand phrase. What we usually mean by fate is what we least understand, that is to say, ourselves, that subversive, unknown individual constantly plotting against us, whom, estranged and alienated but still bowing with disgust before his might, we call, for the sake of simplicity, fate. And if I wish to see my life not only as a series of chance events following the chance happening of my birth (a rather unworthy one), but rather as a sequence of recognitions (a view that satisfies my pride, my pride at least), then the question that took shape in the presence of Dr. Oblath or perhaps with his assistance, "*to view my existence in the context of your potentiality,*" was modified in light of the sequence of recognitions and the shadow of time past, and it was modified once and finally to: "*to view your nonexistence in the context of the necessary and fundamental liquidation of my existence,*" because this is the only way to make sense of all that happened, what I did, what others did to me, this is the only way to make sense of my senseless life, and give sense to my continuing what I have started, to live and to write, it's all the same, both together, for the pen is my spade; when I look ahead I only look back, when I stare at the paper I only see the past: *she crossed that bluish green carpet as if she were crossing the sea* because she wanted to talk to me, for she found out that I was "B.," author and literary translator, one of whose "works" she had read, and which she definitely wanted to discuss with me, she said, and we talked and talked until we talked ourselves into bed – Good God! – and continued to talk even then, uninterrupted. Yes, I do remember, she started by asking if I were serious about what I said during a heated discussion earlier. I don't know what I said, I answered, and I really didn't know, for I said so many things and I was about to take French leave (as the English say) because I was annoyed and bored by the earlier discussion in the course of which I said those things driven by my customary and hated urge to speak, that urge to speak that usually comes upon me when I'd most like to be silent. In these circumstances my urge to speak is nothing but noisy silence, articulated silence, if I may be allowed to take the modest paradox a step further. I asked her, then, to refresh my memory, and she delineated a few points of departure in a muffled, breaking voice, almost strictly, aggressively, and all in all with a certain dark, nervous excitement – a sexual overture transposed or sublimated into the intellectual sphere or quite simply disguised as an intellectual sphere – I thought clumsily with that sense of infallibility with which one usually practices one's fallibility, with that doomed blindness with which we never recognize the consequence of the moment, the consistency in chance events, the clash in a meeting out of which at least one participant will have to drag himself as a cripple. A sexual overture, I thought naturally and shamelessly, as we transpose or sublimate or quite simply disguise our own sexual overtures. Yes, especially nowadays in my deep dark night, I see rather than hear that party's conversation; I see melancholy faces around me, but only as so many theatrical masks, each in its own role: the weeping and the laughing; the wolf and the sheep, the monkey, the bear and the crocodile. And this menagerie murmured quietly as if in a large, primeval swamp where the players as in an Aesop horror fable draw the final lesson and someone comes up with the melancholy idea that everyone should tell *where he was;* then, as from a passing cloud that had already long ago spent its force, the muffled drops of names begin to fall: Hauthausen, the Don elbow, Recsk, Siberia, the Collection Camp, Ravensbruck, Hain Street, Andrassy Street 60, the women of the deportation villages, of the Post Fifty-six prisons, Buchenwald, Kistavesa . . . I was already beginning to dread my turn but, fortunately, I was preempted . . . "Auschwitz," said someone in the modest yet self-assured voice of a victor, and the whole company nodded. "Unbeatable," said our host with a partly envious, partly resentful, but in the final analysis still approving smile of recognition. Then the subject of a then-fashionable book came up and a sentence from that book, fashionable then, even today, and what's more, fashionable probably forever, which its author uttered after the appropriate, but of course totally futile, clearing of his throat with broken voice muffled – by emotion: "Auschwitz cannot be explained." He said it thus; tersely, emotionally, and with a quiet, broken voice. I remember my astonishment at how this group of people, most of whom were quite clever, accepted this idiotically simplistic sentence, weighed it, discussed it, looking this way and that from behind the masks, cunningly or hesitantly or with uncomprehendingly blinking eyes, as if this declarative sentence, suffocating all declaration in its gestation, would actually say something. And yet, it doesn't take a Wittgenstein to notice that the sentence is faulty even from the point of pure linguistic logic; at most, it reflects some hopes, a false or childishly honest morality, and a slew of suppressed complexes; and from that, it has no information value whatsoever. I believe I actually said this, and then I just talked and talked, unstoppably, as if possessed by logomania, occasionally noticing a woman's eyes glued to me as if they were trying to draw forth a spring (fountain) from me: that's what I remembered in that forced flow of speechifying, hasty, probably mistaken, reflecting, at best, some desires and suppressed complexes. This, I said, is what I remembered. The eyes belonged to her; my wife to be, but first my lover, whom I first met only after this discussion, when, exhausted and embarrassed and forgetting everything, I was about to take French leave as the English put it. She crossed a bluish green carpet as if crossing the sea. I no longer remember what I said, I probably voiced my opinion, which probably hasn't changed much, if any, since then. I don't believe it has changed at all, only that nowadays I rarely voice my opinions, perhaps because of the doubts I have concerning them; and then, again, why and to whom should I voice my opinions, and most of all where? After all, I don't continually lodge in a Central Mountains resort to pass the nonpassing time in the company of Dr. Oblath and his intellectual ilk, voicing opinions; no, not in the least; usually, or almost always, I stay in the room – heaven forgive, I almost said the fourteenth-floor flat of a prefab apartment building, sunburned or wind buffeted (sometimes both at the same time). There I live and occasionally I look up at the glorious air or the clouds into which I keep digging my grave with my pen, diligently, like a forced laborer, whom they order every day to dig deeper with his spade so that he play death on his violin with a darker, sweeter voice; here I could only voice my opinion to the rattling water pipes, the clattering heat pumps, or the neighbor's howling, here in this prefab apartment building in the heart – nay, not heart, but the intestines of Jozsefvaros. This building, arising from the squat suburb, is so out of place, so shocking, as an oversized protruding false limb. But from my windows I can at least catch a glimpse – surprise, surprise – behind a still-existing old fence of a wretched garden's wretched secrets, which used to greatly excite me when I was a child but no longer excite me now; in fact they definitely bore me, as does the idea that due to certain circumstances (my divorce, my predilection for the worst possible but not necessarily simplest solutions, and the fact that I'm not exactly swimming in money) I ended up back here where I spent a few sad summer and winter vacations of my childhood, where I acquired a few sad childhood experiences. The idea, thus, that I'm living here again, as long as I have to live, fourteen floors above my childhood, inevitably, consequently, and by now exclusively to my annoyance, my totally superfluous childhood memories descend upon me once in a while. I say superfluous, for these memories have long accomplished what they had to set out to do: their insidious, secret, all-encompassing, all-destroying, all-devouring ratwork; they should really leave me in peace now.

But to return – where to? – to my opinions – Good God! – I probably said that the sentence "Auschwitz cannot be explained" is faulty simply from a formal point of view, for anything that *is* has an explanation, even if by necessity a merely self-serving, faulty, so-so explanation. It is, however, a fact that all facts have at least two lives: one factual, the other, shall we say, spiritual, the latter of which is nothing more than an explanation or explanations or, rather, the slew of overexplaining, that is to say, in the final analysis, annihilating, but at least confiscatory explanations of the given fact. By way of that wretched sentence "Auschwitz cannot be explained" is the wretched author explaining that we should be silent concerning Auschwitz, that Auschwitz doesn't exist, or, rather, that it didn't, for the only facts that cannot be explained are those that don't or didn't exist. However, I most likely continued my train of thought, Auschwitz did exist, or, rather, *does* exist, and can, therefore, be explained; what could not be explained is that no Auschwitz ever existed, that is to say, one can't find an explanation for the possibility that Auschwitz didn't exist, hadn't occurred, that the state of facts labeled Auschwitz hadn't been the materialization of a *Weltgeist* (to give credit to Dr. Oblath herewith), yes, indeed, it is precisely the absence of Auschwitz that could not be explained. Consequently, Auschwitz must have been hanging in the air for a long, long time, centuries, perhaps like a dark fruit slowly ripening in the sparkling rays of innumerable ignominious deeds, waiting to finally drop on one's head. After all, what is, is; and its very existence is necessitated by the fact that it is. The history of the world is the image and deed of cognition (to quote H.), because to see the world as a series of arbitrary chance occurrences would be a rather unworthy view of the world (to quote myself). Let us not forget, therefore, that whoever observes the world cognitively, that person will be flawed cognitively by the world: the two are mutually dependent upon each other. Thus spoke H. again, not H. Führer and Chancellor but H. larger than life-sized visionary, philosopher, court jester, headwaiter of select delicacies to all Führers, Chancellors, and other sundry titled usurpers. He is, I am afraid, entirely right to boot, only that we have to carefully examine the details as to what kind of *cognition* it is whose image and deeds world history is comprised of and, further, as to *whose* cognition the worldviews' rationality reflect so that they can mutually determine each other – as they have, unfortunately, done from time immemorial. I could have said about Auschwitz (and I probably did say it, because it was my opinion then as it is now) that the explanation is contained in individual lives and exclusively in individual lives, nowhere else. Accordingly, Auschwitz is the image and deeds of individual lives in my opinion, seen under the emblem of a particular organization. If all of mankind commences to dream, Moosbrugger is bound to be born, that attractive lust-murderer we read of in Musil's *The Man Without Qualities*. That's what I probably said. Yes, the totality of individual lives and the technique of administering the whole thing, that's the explanation, no more, nothing else: *all that is possible will happen, only that which is possible happens* says K., the great, sad sage who already precisely deduced from individual lives what it would be like when criminal madmen viewed the world rationally and the world, in return, viewed *them* rationally – obeyed them, that is. And don't tell me, I probably added, that this explanation is a tautology, explaining facts with facts, because, yes, indeed, this *is* the explanation. I know how difficult it is for you to accept the fact, I probably said, that common criminals rule us, it's difficult even though on other occasions you call them common criminals and recognize them as such; still, when a criminal madman ends up not in an insane asylum or maximum security prison but in the Chancery or some other substantial domicile, you immediately start to search for some meaning, you start to look for the original, the extraordinary, the – you don't dare say it aloud but say it in secret – for the greatness in him so that you won't be forced to see yourselves as dwarfs and world history as incomprehensible. I probably said all that, and, yes, that you do this so that you can see the world rationally and be seen by the world rationally. And all this is perfectly understandable, what's more, perfectly justifiable, even if your methodology is neither as "scientific" nor as "objective" as you wish to believe. It's neither: it's only lyricism and moralizing intended to reinstate a rational, that is to say, sufferable world order, enabling those exiled from this world to return, to sneak back through front and back doors into the world, that is to say, those who wish to do so and who believe that the world is going to be a habitable place for people . . . but that's a different issue, I must have said. The only problem is that this is how legends are born; from these types of "objective" lyrical works, such "scientific" horror novels, we learn that the great man had an exceptional tactical sense, as if to say that not every paranoid and manic madman deceived and despoiled his environment and their physicians by means of his exceptional sense of tactics. And then, to say that the social situation was this or that and that the international political situation was this or that and, moreover, that philosophy and music and other artistic hocus-pocus corrupted people's ways of thinking . . . but most of all to say that the great man, after all – call a spade a spade – was a great man, that there was something seductive, something briefly fascinating, something demonic, yes, demonic about him; something that simply couldn't be resisted – especially not if we didn't want to resist it since we were on a search precisely for demons. For a long time we have needed a demon for our disgusting affairs, to live out our disgusting desires – needless to say, a demon who can be persuaded that *he* is the demon, who takes all our demonlike qualities upon his shoulders, like an Antichrist shouldering his iron cross, and doesn't insultingly escape our claws to prematurely hang himself like Stravrozin. Yes, those whom you recognize as common criminal madmen and label as such you begin to apotheosize the minute one gets his hands on the scepter and the orb, apotheosize him, albeit insultingly; you enumerate objective circumstances, you tell where he was right *objectively,* where he was wrong *subjectively;* what one can understand *objectively,* what not *subjectively;* what intrigues were going on in the background, what interests were playing a role; and you never run out of explanations just to save your souls and whatever else is salvageable, simply to be able to see common robbery, murder, and kidnapping, to which we all are or were participants one way or another, on the grand spectacular opera-house stage of world history. All of us were, I probably said, all of us sitting here, and that, yes, you are rescuing partial truths, fishing them out of the sea after the great shipwreck where *everything has broken,* yes, but in order to avoid seeing the chasm gaping open in front of you, behind you, under you, and everywhere, I must have said, you call the void, the nothing, that is to say, our genuine situation, that which you serve, and the nature of power, the nature of all power, which by itself is neither necessary nor superfluous, but simply a question of decision, individual decisions made or not made, neither satanic nor unfathomable and fascinatingly subtle, nor grandly spellbinding; no, even during its periods of common, criminal, stupid, murderous, hysterical, or grand accomplishments, you can only view it as well organized at best, I must have said, yes, and as sincere, for ever since the factories of murder have opened their gates here and yonder and at so many locations, there came an end to all sincerity that could be taken seriously, at least where it concerns the concept of power, any sort of power. And please stop saying, I most probably said, that Auschwitz cannot be explained, that Auschwitz is the product of irrational, incomprehensible forces, because there is always a rational explanation for wrongdoing: it's quite possible that Satan himself, like Iago, is irrational; his creations, however, are rational creatures indeed; their every action is as soluble as a mathematical formula: it can be solved by reference to an interest, greed, sloth, desire for power, lust, or cowardice; to one or another self-indulgence, and if to nothing else then, finally to some madmen, paranoia, sadism, lust, masochism, demiurgic or other megalomania, necrophilia or to – what do I know – some other perversity or perhaps to all of them simultaneously. On the other hand, I then probably said, and this is important, what is *really* irrational and what truly cannot be explained is not evil but, contrarily, the good. For that very reason I am no longer interested in Führers, Chancellors, or other sundry titled usurpers, regardless of how many interesting details you muster concerning their spiritual worlds; no, instead of the lives of dictators, it is, exclusively and for a long time now, the lives of the saints that interest me. This is what I find interesting and incomprehensible, this is what I cannot find a rational explanation for. And even Auschwitz – although this sounds like black humor – especially Auschwitz proved to be a most fruitful field of exploration in this respect. Let me tell you a story, even if you are sick and tired of listening: listen and then explain it to me if you can. I'll be short – I am facing a bunch of veterans for whom a shorthand sketch of the setting will suffice: camp, winter, the transportation of the sick, ox-drawn carriages, and a one-day portion of cold food allowance, even though the road will last who knows how many days. The food portions are measured in units of ten, and as I lay on the piece of wood promoted to a stretcher, my dog eyes are glued to a man, or rather a skeleton, referred to as the Professor, I don't quite know why, who holds my portion as well. The assignments, the numbers don't match, of course, so there are shouts, confusion, a kick, and then I feel myself lifted up and placed in front of the next wagon . . . I see neither the "Professor" nor my ration; this suffices to give you exact picture of the situation. You also know how I felt: first and foremost, I couldn't feed my eternal torturer, hunger, that estranged, angrily demanding beast, hope, which up until now continued to drum, albeit muffled and dull, that in spite of everything there was still a chance for surviving. The problem was that without my food allotment the question of survival appeared to be purely academic, while – at the same time I explained to myself with cold detachment – that same portion doubled the "Professor's" chances for survival. This is what I pondered, not particularly joyfully but all the more rationally. But lo and behold, what did I see in a few minutes? Shouting and his eyes restlessly searching, the "Professor" was unsteadily heading for me, carrying a single portion of the cold food allotment, and when he caught sight of me on the stretcher, he quickly put the food in my stomach; I wanted to say something, and it seems that my total surprise screamed unabashedly from my face, because as he quickly headed back – if they didn't find him in his place they'd kill him – he replied with recognizable disgust on his moribund face: "Well, what did you expect . . . ?" That's it for the story, and even if it's true that I don't wish to view my life merely as an arbitrary chance of birth followed by a series of other arbitrary chances because that would be a rather unworthy view of life, I want to view my life even less as a series of attempts to keep me alive, which, perhaps, would be an even less worthy view: yet it is a fact that, for example, the Professor did what he did in order to keep me alive, that is to say, viewing the event from my point of view, for he, probably, was motivated by something entirely different. He probably acted primarily in the interest of his own survival and only secondarily for mine. And this here is the question, this is what I'd like you to answer if you can: why did he do it? But don't try to answer in words, for we all know that under certain circumstances at a particular temperature, metaphorically speaking, words lose their form, their context, their signification; they simply turn to naught; so that in this vaporized state only deeds, sheer deeds show any tendency to remain concrete; it is only the deeds that we can take into our hands, so to say, and examine like pieces of mute rocks, like crystal. And if we go on the assumption – and here, won't you agree, we can't go on any other – that, after all, in a concentration camp, but also in all circumstances, the total physical and mental deterioration and the resulting almost chronic atrophying of one's ability to judge are governed by and large solely by one's desire for survival, and, further, if we consider that the "Professor" was given two chances for survival and that he *threw away* this double chance – that is, to be precise, the chance beyond his chance, which actually would have been someone else's chance – that would indicate that the acceptance of that second chance would have assimilated the *only chance he* had enabling him to live and survive and that, accordingly, there *is* something – and, again, I beg you, don't try to label it – there exists a pristine concept untainted by all strange material circumstances: our bodies, our souls, our hearts; an idea that exists in the minds of all of us as an identical concept, yes, an idea whose preservation, protection, constituted his, the "Professor's" *only genuine chance* for survival. The chance for survival without adherence to this idea was no chance at all for him, because without the preservation, the pristine, undisturbed valuation of this concept, he did not wish to, or what's more, probably could *not* live. Yes, indeed, I believe there is no explanation for this because it is not rational, not in comparison with the concrete rationality of the daily food ration, which would serve the avoidance of the finality of the final solution called concentration camp, that is to say, it would serve it if service would clash against the resistance of an ethereal concept sweeping away even the drive for life. And that, in my opinion, is a very important testimony to that great metabolism of fate which really constitutes life, much, much more important than any commonplaces and rational nightmares any Führer, Chancellor, or other sundry titled usurper could or would serve up. This is what I probably said . . . But I am tired of my stories, although I can't deny them and can't be silent about them, because it is my duty to tell them, albeit I don't know why it's my duty, or more precisely, why I feel it's my duty, especially since, of course, I have no duty whatsoever, no business, since my business here on earth had come to an end and I have only one single business to attend to, as we all know, one that really doesn't depend on me, certainly not; and now, as I reflect on my stories from afar, meditatively, as on the smoke curling up from my cigarette, I see the eyes of a woman glued on me as if she wanted to burst open a well within me, and in light of these eyes I suddenly understand, fully understand, and almost see how the skein of stories gradually turns into woven yarn, and from colorful yarn into soft slings, which I wave around the soft shiny hair, waist, breast, and neck of my (then future, now former) wife, before that, lover, lying in my bed with her head resting on my chest. I am entangling her, tying her to myself, turning, swirling like two brightly colored, agile circus performers, who, in the end, take their bows, deathly pale and empty-handed before a malicious spectator – before failure. But, yes, indeed, *one has to, at least, strive for failure,* says that scientist in Thomas Bernland, because failure and failure alone remains as the one single accomplishable experience, say I. Thus, I, too, am striving for failure, if strive I must, and I must because I live and write and both are strives, life a rather blind one, writing more of a seeing strive and as such a different striving from life. Perhaps the strive in writing is striving to see what life's strive is, and for that reason, since it can't do any differently, it retells life, repeats life as if it were life as well, even though it is not, quite fundamentally, quite incomparably it is not, and as such its failure is fundamentally assured as soon as we begin to write and write of life. And now when I seek the answers to those final grand questions this deep dark night sent by lights, sounds, and my piercing pain, I know full well that there is only one possible final and grand answer to all final and grand questions, one that solves everything because it silences all questions and all questioners. In the final analysis this is the only possible solution for us; this is the final goal of all our efforts, even if we ignore it and don't strive for it at all, because then we wouldn't strive at all, although as far as I am concerned I don't see the point of beating around the bush . . . still – good God – as I was reflecting, counting my life here, and asking myself why on earth I was doing it aside from the fact that I had to work, maniacally, with crazed diligence, unceasingly, because, obviously, there are some most serious connections between my existence and my life: I am probably driven by some secret hope of my secret strive; that is to say, in order to know and have that hope once, I'll probably continue to write, maniacally, with crazed diligence and unceasingly, until I discover it . . . and then what would be the point of writing?

When my wife (future and former) later asked me as we walked the dim and less dim streets what appellation I would give that certain pristine concept not contaminated by any foreign substance of which I earlier spoke in connection with the "Professor," whom, incidentally, she found to be "a very moving character" and whom she said she hoped to meet in some of my works, I passed over her remark as over a beauty flaw that cannot be allowed to disturb the magic – at least momentarily – while the magic lasts. I passed over it with my eyes closed, so to say, and responded without any hesitation that in my opinion that concept was freedom, and that it is first and foremost freedom because the "Professor" did not do what he had to do, what, in other words, he should have done according to the rational demands of hunger, the instinct for survival, and the madness and the governing rules of the blood pact of hunger, survival instinct, and madness. He didn't do what he had to do but did something else in spite of everything, something that he didn't have to do and what no one in his right mind expected him to do. My wife (she wasn't my wife yet then) fell silent for a little while and then spoke suddenly; I still remember her face lifted to mine and illuminated by the passing lights of the night, glowing and sparkling softly like glass, like a picture from the thirties, and I remember her voice too, trembling with emotion and the excitement of taking courage – at least I believed it to be that then, and perhaps it was, indeed, the case, but then again, why should it have been, for nothing ever is what we believe it to be or want to believe it to be; the world is not our imagination but our nightmare, full of inconceivable surprises – she said suddenly that I must be very lonely and very sad and very inexperienced in spite of all my experiences to have so little trust in man, yes, that I have to fabricate experiences in order to explain a natural (yes, she indeed said *natural*), honorable human gesture. I remember how startled I was by those words, those absolutely dilettantish and in their untenability so profound remarks. I remember, yes, I do remember her subsequent smile, first rather timid, then turning inquisitive, and then almost immediately intimate, this facial sequence which I have often tried to recreate for myself, because in a certain sense it has always delighted me, first pleasurably so, later, when I no longer succeeded in recreating it, painfully – that is to say, my reaction was caused first by its reality, then by its absence, as it's usually the case and the way, it seems, it must be because it never happens otherwise; I remember it all, I remember my thickening and almost unpleasantly immediate and suddenly confusing feelings, and, even more so, her question, which was whether or not she may take my arm. Of course, I answered.

At this point, though, I should tell you the way I lived in those days so that I may understand and recognize what I must understand and recognize: that is, how did that moment differ from other similar moments that, just like this one, determined that soon I will take a woman to bed. I said the moment determined, or made me determine, because even though, admittedly – nothing is more obviously obvious – it's true that in such decisions I, too, am a participant – or at least appear to be that, still, the occasion never presents itself as a decision-making process, but contrarily as an adventure thwarting even the possibility of decision making, like a chasm opening up before my feet as the sound of my blood pulsating like a waterfall mutes any other considerations within me. I am perfectly aware of the customary outcome of the adventure well ahead of time so that, as far as the relevant decision making is concerned, I would certainly not decide in favor of such an adventure were it in my power to do so. But, perhaps, it's precisely this contradiction, this chasm that attracts me.

I don't know; I just don't know. For this had happened to me before – the same thing, in the same way, so that I have to assume the presence of some sort of regularity from its regular occurrences: a woman quietly and modestly asks for admittance, she asks with a timid smile, hushed movement, almost as if in the archaic disguise of a barefooted maidservant with flowing hair. She asks admittance to my – how shall I say it without using banalities, those banalities that I can't avoid, though, because what else shall I say since that ancient tag has worked since time immemorial and has worked quite excellently – she asks for admittance, then, to my *ultimum moriens,* that is to say, to my heart; once admitted, she looks around with a pleasant and curious smile on her lips, she touches everything with gentle hands, dusts here or there, airs out musty corners, throws away a few things and replaces them with a few of her own belongings; neatly, carefully, and irresistibly she makes herself at home until, finally, I find myself displaced, totally excluded so that nervously, like an exiled stranger, I avoid my own heart, which beckons to me from afar with closed gates, like other people's cozy homes to the homeless. Frequently, the only way I can move back is when I arrive, hand in hand, with another woman and establish *her* there.

All of these I only pondered thoroughly after the conclusion of my rather lengthy, progressively painful, and endlessly lasting relationship, I pondered, usually, so to say, as befits my vocation as author and literary translator; that relationship took a lot out of me, or, at least I believed that to be the case then, and since I perceived it to constitute a danger to my personal freedom necessary, nay, essential for my work, it prompted me to be cautious with regard to future relationships and also to reflect further. This happened mostly because I had to admit that the reacquisition of my longed-for freedom did not bestow the enthusiasm for work I expected from this change; quite the contrary, in shock I had to admit that while I was simply struggling for freedom, indecisively breaking up one minute, returning the next, I was actually working more vigorously, I could say angrily, and consequently with more results than later when I was free once again but when this freedom merely filled me with emptiness and boredom. Much later but in the same manner, another condition, namely happiness, which I experienced during our relationship and in the course of my relationship to my wife, also taught me that happiness, too, has an adverse effect on my work. As a consequence I first examined my work as to what it actually is and why it always places such exhausting, often even impossible, almost suicidal demands on me. And even though I was still far, far away from the genuine realization of the nature of my work – good God – which in the final analysis is nothing but digging, the continued, concluding digging of the grave that others have started to dig for me in the air, I did recognize at least that much: that while I worked, I was; if I didn't, who knows whether I'd be or *could be;* thus there were very serious connections between my existence and my work, for which one apparent prerequisite (I believed this regardless of how sadly it reflected on me, because I could assume no differently) was *unhappiness*. But, of course, I am not talking of the type of unhappiness that would deprive me of the possibility to work, such as sickness, homelessness, misery, imprisonment, or the like, no, I mean that species of unhappiness that can only be bestowed upon me by women. Therefore, and especially because in those days I was reading Schopenhauer's essay "Über die anscheinende Absichtlichkeit im Schiksale der Einzelnen" in one of the volumes of his *Parergo and Paralipomena* – I got my hands on those volumes during the library liquidation following the great national unrest and the subsequent wave of dissidents; I acquired them in an antiquarian shop, so inexpensively that even I was able to pay the price for these four thick volumes that have survived all censorship, book burning, all sorts of biblio-Auschwitzes – therefore, as I said, I couldn't entirely exclude the possibility that, to use the most unfashionable expression of a totally unfashionable psychoanalysis, I had some sort of an Oedipal complex, which, taking the not particularly ordered circumstances of my adolescence into consideration, wouldn't be all that surprising. The only question, then, I asked myself, was whether I was determined by a father-son or a mother-son role (not as an exclusive determinant, though, but the mere potentiality of this self-analysis is more than hopeful, I thought). I answered myself by saying that my behavior reflects – here and there – the mother-son, the rejected mother-son role. I went so far as to fabricate a theory concerning that; my early notes bear testimony to it. According to this, the rejected father-son tends to be more transcendentally problematic; the rejected mother-son, on the other hand (and I had to postulate myself to be one), tends to be of more sensitive, formable, and malleable material, receptive to plasticity; the first I thought to be found in Kafka, the second in Proust or Joseph Roth. And even though this theory probably rests on very shaky grounds, and nowadays I would not only be careful not to write it down but even to raise it as a subject for discussion, all the more so since it simply no longer interests me – oh, I'm well beyond that, and if I remember it at all, I remember it as a short, hesitant, and aimless step toward true clairvoyance, that is to say, on the long, long road of self-conscious self-annihilation, which will take who knows how long. At any rate it's a fact – how shall I say it – that the beneficial effects of this theory streamed from me into my work, then noxious effects from my work into me, so that one could deduce – if not from my fate, then definitely from the apparent intentionality of my behavior in those days – that I surreptitiously raised and really created the rejected mother-son situation and role presumably because of the attendant particular – if I weren't embarrassed I'd even say pleasurable pain – which, it seems, I absolutely needed on account of my work (of course, that is along with freedom, which I needed first and foremost). Yes, indeed, it seems that in the final analysis I discover creative powers in pain, with no regard whatsoever to the price and regardless of the fact that, perchance, in this case the creative power is simply a form of common compensation; what's important still is that it does take form and that on account of the pain I live some sort of truth, and if I didn't live it, who knows, it may leave me cold. This way, however, the image of pain fuses intimately and eternally with the face of life within me – with life's most accurate face, I am entirely certain. This therefore explains why my energy for work diminished when I was in full possession of my freedom but increased during periods of struggle for my freedom and in the midst of sundry spiritual pain. Apparently the neurosis triggered by (or triggering) my complex affects me in such a way that when it is laid to rest or diminishing, so is my desire to work; if, on the other hand, I experience a new trauma, which ignites my sleeping neurosis, my desire to work is also rekindled. This is perfectly clear and simple; therefore, one would think, all one would have to do is ensure the continuous flow of causes to trigger the process which would then continue to fuel the fire of my work unceasingly – I phrased this so sharply that its impossibility should become immediately obvious – because as soon as I completed this self-analysis, I eliminated the complex; moreover, I naturally came to despise it, to be precise, despite not only my complex but myself as well, myself who feeds this complex and role-acts even before nourishing this particularly ridiculous infantile complex that attests to psychological immaturity, inadmissible oversensitivity, even though I hate nothing more than infantilism. Thus I was at least cured of this particular complex or, more precisely, I declared myself cured, not, of course, so much in the interest of my health as for the sake of regaining my self-respect. As a result, when I next entered a relationship with a woman, I set the condition (which may sound cruel but is very practical) that the term "love" and all its synonyms must never be spoken, and that our affair can continue only while we – singly or jointly – do not fall in love with each other. The second such an unfortunate turn of events takes place – concerning either partner or God forbid even both – we must immediately terminate the relationship. My partner in those days, who was also recovering from a serious love-accident, accepted this condition without much ado (or so it appeared), albeit the tranquillity of our relationship, I have no doubt, most likely would have disturbed or probably even destroyed the affair had it not been that I met my former (or rather future) wife then, which, for me at least, provided the radical solution. In those days I was still renting a room, which undeniably appeared absurd in light of the fact that we have entered the second decade of consolidation when most of my friends and acquaintances – whatever I call them – have acquired their own homes, albeit usually at the price of strokes, diabetes, eternal ulcers, physical-psychological breakdowns, moral or material ruin, or, in the best of cases, merely the total disintegration of family life. What concerns me, I wasn't thinking of such things, or if I did I thought of them as something *not* to think about simply because it would have necessitated a different way of life in the pursuit of money or, rather, the acquisition of money, and that would have entailed such concessions, compromises, and, in general, so much *inconvenience* – even if I kidded myself by saying that it was only temporary, only for the pursuit of a goal – for how can one live even temporarily differently from the way one lives permanently and usually without the temporary life's miserable consequences intruding into one's normal (that is to say, more or less self-determined) way of life, where, after all, we still are in charge, are the rulers and legislators. I thus simply couldn't and also didn't want to take upon myself all these impossibilities, the impossible inconvenience of an apartment search in Hungary, which would have endangered first and foremost my freedom but also my spiritual independence, or more precisely, my independence from external circumstances; therefore, I had to oppose the danger totally, that is to say, with my whole life. And I must admit that my wife, who with persistent and irresistible inquires discovered my circumstances, was right: her questions accompanied by the facial play that had become familiar to me by then and which, I thought, affected me like an unexpected, spectacularly beautiful sunrise. She said that I imprisoned myself for the sake of my freedom. Yes indeed, there was undoubtedly some truth in that. Or, more precisely, this was the truth. The truth was that given the choice of the prison of acquiring an apartment in Hungary or the prison of not owning an apartment in Hungary, I was better suited by the second – by the prison of not owning one – because there I could do as I pleased, live to myself, protected, hidden, and undecayed, until this prison, or if a comparison is called for, this tin can, was opened suddenly and undoubtedly as a result of my wife's magic touch, and revealed itself all of a sudden as unprotected, exposed, decaying, and consequently as untenable, just as, incidentally, my subsequent and present life proved to be untenable and just as, I believe, life in general proves to be untenable when examined in the light of recognition, for it is precisely the untenability of our lives that leads to recognition – and indeed it is why we cannot hold on to it. Yes. I used to live my rental life as if I didn't quite live, in a reduced, temporary, absentminded way (taking only my work seriously), with a never-explained (but therefore probably in no need of explanation) feeling that all I had to do was to pass the time between my two true occupations: the time of my birth and that of my demise. I'll have to pass that undetermined waiting period somehow (possibly with work), even though this waiting period is the only time I have, this is the only time I can be accountable for, I don't know, though, to whom and why, perhaps to myself above all, so that I would recognize what I still have to recognize and accomplish what I still can accomplish. In the second place I'll have to be accountable to everyone, that is to say, for no one or anyone who will be ashamed because of us and (perhaps) for us, since I can't be accountable for time before my birth or after my death, if, at any rate, these conditions have anything to do with my own singular time. And now that I am pondering my rental life with cold objectivity but not devoid of a certain sentimentality, lengthily and agonizingly in the light of the night descending upon me, I seem to suddenly recognize its prototype, namely, I seem to recognize it in my camp life, not that many years ago yet an eternity away. To be precise, I saw it in that portion of my camp life which no longer was camp life per se, but only in the sense that the liberating soldiers took the place of camp prison guards, yet it was still camp life because I still lived in a camp. It happened on the second day of this situational change (that is, the exchange of liberating soldiers for the camp prison guards) as I was lying in the Saal, that is to say, the large hall of the hospital barracks, because, to put it mildly, I was sick, which by itself didn't of course explain the fact that I was lying in the hospital barracks. However, as a result of a coincidence of certain events that took the shape of an instance of good luck, barely more surprising than the bad luck I have grown accustomed to, I lay in the hospital barracks. The next morning, then, I left the Saal and ambled toward the so-called lavatory, and as I opened the door and started to head toward the sink or perhaps the toilet first, all of a sudden – and I can't find a more appropriate phrase than this abused old one because literally that was what happened – all of a sudden my feet were rooted to the ground, because *there was a German soldier standing at the sink and at my entrance he slowly turned his head toward me*. Before I collapsed, kicked over, wet my pants in fear, who knows what else, I noticed a gesture through the black-gray mist of my terror: it was the gesture of the German soldier's hand motioning me to the sink; I noticed a rag which the German soldier was holding in his hand and also a smile – the smile of a German soldier. All this added up, I gradually understood, to the recognition that *the German soldier was simply cleaning the sink* and that his smile simply expressed his eagerness to assist me, and that *he was cleaning the sink for me,* which is to say that the world had turned topsy-turvy or that the world hadn't changed at all except for the not entirely dismissible fact that yesterday I was the vanquished but today it was he. This recognition only partially put an end to my fear in that the immediate experience gradually tamed my fear into a long-lasting and unshakable suspicion; it ripened it to a worldview, so to say, which then bestowed a particular flavor to my subsequent life in camp, for I lived there for a long time, as a free occupant of the camp: it was the flavor of an unforgettably sweet and cautious experience of life regained. I lived, admittedly, but I lived in such a way that *the Germans might return at any time;* thus I didn't quite live. Yes, I must believe that, while probably unconsciously by then and determined by circumstances, giving in to the demands for shelter, still, after all, I was prolonging this experience, the sweet and cautious experience of my life in the freed camp, during my life as a renter. I was prolonging the experience of this life unencumbered by no pre- and post-recognition burdens, by the burden of life itself: albeit I live in a way that the Germans may return at any time. And if I bestow any theoretical interpretation on this concept or way of life or whatever you call it, it all of a sudden ceases to be impossible because it is a fact that, theoretically speaking, the Germans may indeed return at any time: *der Tod ist ein Meister aus Deutschland, sein Auge ist blau,* "Death is a blue-eyed German maistro and magister," he may come at any time, wherever he may find you, he'll take aim and he never misses: *er trifft dich genau.* Thus, I lived my rental life in such a way that I didn't quite live, and, undeniably, this was not quite life; it was, rather, functioning, yes, *surviving* to be more precise.

It is obvious that all this left lasting marks upon me. I presume the roots of my particularly obvious quirks also rest here. I believe I should mention, for example, my relationship with possessions here, this nonexisting relationship of negation. I don't believe and can't even imagine that this negativity is inborn, some sort of birth defect, for how could I then explain my desperate clinging to my small possessions (books) or, for that matter, to my most important possession: myself, the fact that I have always, decisively, one could almost say radically, protected and continue to protect the possession I consider most important, myself, from all forms of practical self-destruction, which is not a result of my full choice, on one hand, and from any cheap and generic seduction of sundry social ideas on the other, the latter of which I could, incidentally, number among species of practical self-destruction. I have protected and continue to protect myself, and progressively more so, even if I'm only saving myself for another sort of destruction: No, I have no doubts that my negative relationship with possessions was determined by the survival of my survival instinct, this particular and in a certain sense not entirely unproductive but, of course, unfortunately untenable mode of existence that made my living in a rented room self-explanatory. In the rented room, which I first occupied during those darkest of years, which, according to the mad rules of hell, we unceasingly had to declare louder and more enthusiastically as the brightest epoch, I was received almost as a savior because my presence seemed to provide protection from requisition, takeover, repossession, lease, etc., etc., of the only available room of this incidentally quite pleasing flat, nestled in one of the Buda side streets. For that reason, I had to pay only symbolic rent, so to say, which, in the consequent years, was raised only symbolically, so to say. In this rental situation, I never thought of possessions, either at a time when I couldn't have nor later when I could have or even should have; here I wasn't threatened by the dangers concomitant to ownership: the painful and hopeless negotiations necessitated by a break in pipes, ceilings, or other surfaces; the considerations necessitated by ownership such as whether or not the possessions are satisfying and whether or not one shouldn't acquire further or at least more satisfying property – at the cost, of course, of selling our existing and not satisfying property at the best possible price. No, the frightening image of change simply couldn't have arisen in my head; this itchy stimulus that would always place me in front of a never-ending series of imaginary choices would bother me constantly and deceive me with the promise that I could change my living here to living there, and could exchange my prefab flat (after, of course, the price, the necessary running around, paying up front, official business, and other sundry unimaginable complications had been dispensed with) for a more satisfying one, even if I have no idea what would satisfy me more since I don't even know my own wishes. I hadn't even mentioned furnishings, the unsolvable problem of furnishings, as a result of which my prefab abode is still, after all these years, not satisfactorily furnished. I simply don't know how to furnish my flat. I have no notion of a flat furnishable for me; I have no idea what kind of a flat I'd like to have and what objects I'd like to see in it. When I was renting, all pieces of furniture, all objects, were the property of the owners; they expected me to move in, everything provided and arranged; and during those long, long years that I spent in their home the idea never occurred to me to ever rearrange any of the pieces, much less to exchange them for some other objects or to cluster them with some other objects. The simple reason was that, let's assume, I noticed an object, desired to own it, bought it (aside from books, my books that I placed in the wardrobe, there, and when that was full, on the table, and then when there was no more room there, simply on the floor, until my landlord put an additional small bookcase in my room) – but that wasn't the case, I tell you, I didn't wish for any, I didn't buy any, and, most probably, didn't even notice any objects; nothing upsets me as much as a shop window jammed full of objects; such windows literally depress, sadden, even demoralize me. Therefore, as I said, I don't even see them, obviously an indication that I am not likely to have such needs. In this respect, concerning objects, I am satisfied with the bare necessities, as they say, I am probably the happiest when I am placed into a ready-made physical environment where all I have to do is to accept this particular constellation of objects, get to know them, and get used to them. I believe I was born to be a hotel guest, even if those times have changed – I could only be the inhabitant of camps and rented rooms – I noted in my notebooks then, from which I'm now, decades later, copying things into another notebook, surprised somewhat that even back then I was writing down things like that, which would indicate that even then I wasn't entirely blind to my situation, to this untenable situation and the untenability of an untenable life. In those days, I remember, I suffered greatly from a feeling, I should probably say, sadness, which for my personal use I termed "alienation." I have known this feeling from early childhood on, essentially, it has accompanied me throughout life, but in those days it tempted me almost in a frighteningly dangerous way: at night it wouldn't let me sleep, during the day it wouldn't let me work, I was simultaneously tense to the point of bursting and exhausted to the point of impotence. This is a well-researched spiritual malady, not a figment of one's imagination; I, for one, believe that it is essentially based on the reality of the human condition. It usually commences with that often astonished, at other times (especially in those days) unbearably passionate feeling that my whole life is hanging on a thread, not the question of whether I live or die, no, it has nothing to do with death, only and exclusively with life, it's only that it fills me with an image of life's sudden and total uncertainty, its formlessness, so that I am totally uncertain of its reality; yes, indeed, I am seized by a total mistrust toward the doubtful experience of my senses and all that they indicate as being real; all in all, doubts toward the realness of my own and my environment's existence, to which existence, during periods of this experience, or perhaps I should call them assaults, during periods of these assaultlike experiences, then, I am connected to life only by a single thread, and this single thread is my cognition, nothing else. My mind, though, is not only an instant gauge tending to make mistakes and far from perfect, but most of the time it works hesitatingly, with veiled vision, and occasionally barely at all. It only follows my actions in the manner of a man in bed with the flu, only registering the puttering about of another person in the room almost all retroactively, and even though he tries to direct the stranger's moves with an exhausted word here and there, if that other person doesn't listen or doesn't hear him, then he gives up all further efforts with resigned weakness. Yes, this is alienation, the state of being totally alien, a state that, however, does not contain even the most infinitesimal activity of fantasy, a startling roaming imagination; it tortures you with the boredom of routine, everyday things, yes, this is pristine homelessness, albeit a state that knows or teaches nothing of a home, a home deserted or one waiting for me, nothing of, for instance (and this is a question I often asked myself while in this state), what death was like at home. Except, of course, I would answer myself every time, except, of course, I would have to believe in a hereafter then, and the problem is precisely this: I can't even believe in the here and now, least of all when I am in this state when I am forced to ask myself these questions, and then I consider the other, that is to say, the existence of a hereafter, to be just as much an impossibility as the existence of this world; in other words, I don't consider it inconceivable – or for that matter conceivable – that there could be another world, a hereafter; only that if it does exist, it's certain that it doesn't exist *for me* because I am *here*. That is to say, barely here. I live only halfway and that overwhelms me with an ephemeral sense of guilt. At times like this I often tried, try, to sober up, so to say, but all is in vain; I'm afraid I can only enter a relationship with life in the form of some sort of a logical game, just as one plays chess or does calculations on paper, and in some ineffable way some kind of reality emerges from the abstract results. I had a favorite illustration for this in those days, I even wrote it down in my notebook out of which I am copying it now; it is life grabbing two ropes, tying them, sticking one end into the wall, pressing a button, the light going on. "What happens is pure, conscious probability analysis," I wrote, "the results are predictable yet still amazing and in a certain sense inexplicable." "Everything involved is hypothesis, deduction, and probability; there is no certainty anywhere, no evidence," I wrote. "What's my essence, why am I, what's my existence? Searching not even for answers but only for reliable signs is clearly hopeless," I wrote. "My body is foreign to me," I wrote, "that body that sustains me and will, ultimately, kill me." "Perhaps, if there were a single moment in my life when I could synchronize, so to say, with the defortifying activity of my liver and kidneys, the peristaltic activity of my intestines, the breathing of my lungs, the systolic and diastolic doings of my heart as well as the metabolism of my brain with the outside world, the formation of the abstract thoughts of my mind, my cognition's pure knowledge of myself and of everything, and the tyrannical yet merciful presence of my transcendental soul; if just for one second I could *see, know, possess* myself this way – and here, of course, I don't mean possessions, but simply the emergence of my identification, my sameness, which can never, never happen. If, therefore, such a single unrealizable moment would realize itself, that and that alone could put a stop to my sense of alienation – that would teach me to *know,* only then would I know what it means to be. But since this is impossible because cognitively we don't know and will never discover what occasions the cause of our existence, we don't know the purpose of our existence and we don't know why we have to disappear from here once we have been placed here," I wrote. "I don't know," I wrote, "why I have to live this fragmentary existence, which happened to be my lot, instead of a life that perhaps does exist somewhere. Why did I get this lot? This sex, this body, this awareness, this geographic setting, this fate, this language, this history, this rented room?" I wrote. And as I am writing down what I wrote then, suddenly a night long ago comes to life in my memory; a night, a dream, or more precisely, a waking or an awake dream or dreaming awake, I don't know which, but I remember it remarkably well, as if it had happened yesterday. I was startled by some very unusually agitated, never before experienced sense of alienation. Perhaps I didn't wake up but was falling asleep. I can't tell, but it's all the same. It was a radiant night then just as this night is radiant, radiant in its velvety blackness; motionless, mute, and permeated with immense knowledge: I suddenly realized – it would be totally impossible that this sharp, suffering knowledge would suddenly cease and disappear from the face of the world. Yes, and it was as if this recognition was not really my awareness but rather awareness *concerning me,* so that I knew of it but it was not at my disposal, as if, as I said, it were not exclusively my own awareness but an awareness present always and everywhere, which I simply couldn't get rid of and which constantly and pointlessly continued to torture me to death. On the other hand, I felt quite clearly that this painful awareness was not essentially an unhappy one, and if I felt unhappy this particular moment, it was only as the object of this awareness, and as a result of my own impotence in the face of this awareness, as I said, this merciless, eternal, tortuous, but at the same time not at all unhappy awareness. Upon full awakening, or fully falling asleep, for as I said, it really didn't matter which, it became impossible for me not to ascribe it to some mystery, or in other words, it was impossible to ponder the fact that this awareness was part of something else, something that I was a part of, that it didn't belong to my body, nor entirely to my mind, albeit it was transmitted by my mind, and that this awareness was not exclusively mine and that, indeed, this awareness was perhaps the seed of my life that had occasioned and developed the whole thing, that is to say, my very existence. It was impossible for me not to think that; consequently, this awareness came with a responsibility, or task, to reflect, and the awareness that even if I could hypothesize about this task, these notions were still untransgressible, or to be more precise, they were, of course, transgressible but only at the cost of feeling that we have transgressed against a commandment, that is to say, the sense of having sinned. At the same time, and as far as I am concerned this is the most unusual aspect of it, this commandment was not exclusively, how shall I put it, a moral commandment, no, it encompassed an almost mechanical element, a demand even, something to the effect that "one had to build" the world, "one had to copy it," "one had to study it," and, in time, we will have to show – no matter why, or to whom, to anyone who will be ashamed because of us and (perhaps) for us – that man's religious duty is the *understanding* of the world entirely independent of all wretched churches, all wretched creeds; yes, indeed, to show that in the final analysis this and only this (the understanding of the world and the human condition), where I may search for my – what can I say to avoid the unavoidable – my salvation; yes, for what else would I be searching for, since I'm searching, if not my salvation. On the other hand, it also occurred to me that these are thoughts that man *has* to ponder; and that man only ponders these thoughts because of his human condition, because he can't help but ponder them as a result of his condition, and since man's condition, at least in certain aspects, is a predetermined and preordained condition, man can, therefore, only muse and ponder over predetermined thoughts, or at least thoughts on predetermined and preordained subjects, themes, and problems. Consequently, I thought, I should be pondering those thoughts which I shouldn't ponder, albeit I can't remember anymore if, indeed, I pondered any such thoughts; aside from the fact that I thought at all, which *I didn't have to do* since I became a writer and literary translator, which I didn't have to become at all, moreover, which I could only be in spite of all circumstances. I could only be that by circumventing, deceiving circumstances, or by incessant hiding in the labyrinth of circumstances, escaping the bullheaded monster whose swift feet – as if in passing – still crushed me; in spite of these wretched, destructive circumstances, which did not permit any thought in any way, shape, or form, except, perhaps, the thought of a prisoner, that is to say, none at all, those circumstances exulted prison labor only and exclusively; they praised and celebrated it. I could only live, exist among them in secret, so to say, in the way that I denied myself aloud and quietly; fearfully I guarded my velvety black night and my hopeless hopes within me, which many, many years later escaped from my lips, perhaps even for the first time that night when I spoke of the "Professor," occasionally noting the eyes of a woman glued to me as if trying to open up a spring to well up from within me: when I spoke of the existence of a pristine concept not contaminated by any foreign substance such as our bodies, our souls, our monsters, an idea that exists in one and the same form in all our mistakes, yes, an idea that (and that I didn't say, I only thought secretly) perhaps even I could stalk and approximate, or even succeed one day in capturing on paper. It is a thought I think by knowing that I don't have to think, but think it independently and think it even when this thought is directed against me, even if it annihilates me; especially so then, because that will perhaps be the moment when I recognize it; perhaps that will be the litmus test of the thought . . . Yes, that is the way I lived in those days. And now that I am talking about it, I am beginning to understand and recognize what I have to know and recognize. And my answer to the question as to whether or not that particular moment differed from other similar, or rather, not at all similar initial moments of an incipient relationship, I must answer: yes, indeed, it differed fundamentally. Accordingly, at least in a certain sense, I, too, differed from myself fundamentally. For to sum up my life then as a renter, my thoughts, inclinations, motivations, my whole rental survivalhood in those days, everything was ready to make me ripe for a change. I'm sure I am not mistaken in thinking that those were the days I started to assume that I am mistakenly and therefore untenably and intolerably pondering my life. That's when I began to think that I should no longer consider my life simply as a series of arbitrary occurrences following the arbitrary chance of my birth, because this is not only an unworthy, faulty, and therefore untenable or even unbearable view and, above all, a *useless* one; for me at least, it is an unbearably and embarrassingly useless view of life, which I would and must rather see as a series of recognitions that satisfies – if nothing else – my pride. Consequently, the moment that made me decide to go to bed with a woman, that is to say, *with her,* who then became my wife, then my ex-wife, that moment couldn't have been a chance occurrence. For it is quite obvious that everything I wrote down and I prepared had ripened me for a change in state, everything suddenly came to a head that moment, even if I, according to the nature of things, was not able to be aware of it then, yes, even if I can't even remember it, only her face lifted up to mine in the passing light of the night, her face sparkling softly and with the translucence of glass, like a blown-up picture from the silver screen of the thirties. Who would have known the temptations of this promisingly shimmering face? And if I add that, as became clear later, my future (or former) wife was also ready and ripened for a change in state, then I must declare that our meeting was not only not arbitrary but even fated. Yes, indeed, not much time passed and we were already talking of our life together: in truth, though, we both wanted that our own individual fates always remain individual, distanced from everyone else's, and not shareable with anyone else. Thus, whatever we spoke of, it was always circumvention, even if, undoubtedly, it was never intended or recognized as such, in other words, it was not a lie. For how could I have known then what I know better than anything today, namely, that everything I do and everything that happens to me, my states and my occasional changes of state, everything, my whole life – good God! – simply serves as a tool of recognition for me in the series of my recognitions – my marriage, for instance, as the tool of the recognition that I can't live in a marriage. And as it was a decisive recognition in the series of my recognitions, so it was a mortal one for my marriage; if I look at it coldly, from a detached point of view, without having been married I could perhaps never have arrived at this recognition, except, perhaps, in an abstract way of logical deduction. All accusations and self-accusations are thus unavoidable, and my only defenses are the accusations leveled against me: that I contracted my marriage, as I know today, undoubtedly for the sake of my self-destruction, but that when I did marry, I believed it to be for the sake, contrarily, of the future and of happiness, the happiness that my wife and I discussed so often and so timidly and yet so convincingly and decisively, as if we were talking of a secret, almost stern responsibility bestowed upon us. Yes, that's the way it was, and now I see our whole life together, its sounds, events, feelings, in some faded, conflated unity; or rather, this might be quite strange, I hear it like a musical composition under whose texture a theme gradually thickens and matures until, exploding and overwhelming all else, it assumes sole dominance over all: the chief, great, all-consuming theme – *my life's existence viewed in the light of your potential existence; and then, your nonexistence viewed in light of the necessary and fundamentally radical liquidation of my existence.* It was simply a pretense that evening as I spoke of "the Professor" and stringing out "the Professor's" story, or more precisely the lessons of his deed, explained and unveiled it for my wife (who was not my wife then and is no longer my wife now). I was explaining to her, as I said, the probability or lack of probability of possible actions in such a situation, that is to say, in states of totalitarianism. Because, I told her, totalitarianism is a senseless situation and, thus, all situations derivative thereof are senseless, too; albeit, I said, and that's perhaps the most senseless aspect of it all, by sustaining ourselves by mere living we contribute to sustaining totalitarianism in the sense, of course, of clinging to life, wanting to sustain it; this is simply an organism's self-contained, one could say primitive rigmarole, I said. The hypotheses of totalitarianism are naturally founded on Nothing, I said. Choice, exclusion, and other concepts based on these are nonexistent, meaningless concepts and have no reality except their naturalism – such as, for example, one's being pushed into a gas chamber, I said. I'm afraid all this was not particularly amusing conversation, and when I look back upon it now, wondering if I had any reasons other than stating what I had to say, I seem to remember that I didn't. I remember it was my sense of being driven that made me talk, my urge to speak, which a few hours earlier made me speak at the party and, further, my impression that, regardless of how strange or unusual this may be, this woman was interested in what I was saying, this woman walking along with me on her high heels, whom I could only barely see in the middle of the night at my side but whom I didn't really try to see because her image was still within me as she, less than an hour earlier, crossed a bluish green carpet as if sailing across the ocean toward me. Henchman and victim, I said, serve the same purpose in a totalitarian system: they both serve nothing, albeit, naturally, I said, this is not to say that both services are of the same kind. And even though the "Professor's" deed was one performed in totalitarianism, forced by totalitarianism, and as such, in the final analysis, a deed of totalitarianism, that is to say, senselessness, yet the deed itself was still a deed of total victory over total senselessness because it was precisely there in the world of total eradication and destruction that the indestructibility of that concept living in "the Professor," or idée fixe, if you will, could actually become a *revelation*. Then she asked me whether I suffered or perhaps even still suffer from my Jewishness aside from what I had to suffer in the past. I answered that that was something I had to think about. In fact, I have known for a long time, since the first stirrings of a thought in my mind, I have felt that some sort of awful shame is attached to my name and that I have somehow brought this shame along from somewhere, from somewhere I have never been, and that I have carried this sin as my sin even though I have never committed it; this sin pursues me all my life, which life is undoubtedly not my own even though I live it, I suffer from it, and die of it. I think, though, I said, that not everything is necessarily a direct result of my Jewishness, it could simply be a result of myself, my being, my personality, my transcendence, so to say, or the result of others' behavior toward me, my behavior toward others, my and others' general behavior and mutual treatment of each other, in other words, from social conditions and my relationship vis-à-vis these conditions, I said, because, as I said, *judgment doesn't come suddenly; process gradually becomes judgment,* as was written. The subject of my writing came up, too, the particular work which she read and which, as she said, she just *had to* discuss with me. For that reason I, too, have to speak of this particular text and sketch out what kind of writing it was. This writing, actually a longish narrative, was of the type they usually label a "novelette," and it just came out in the haystack of a thick volume of collected short stories and novelettes. It didn't appear without all the ugly and trying prior complications, which I am hesitant to describe because it bores me and disgusts me; besides, such a modest, futile appendage belongs purely to the Hungarian literary scene, this crucifying, humiliating occurrence thriving on exclusion and privilege, preferences and dislikes, confidentially official and confidentially businesslike system of lists, always suspicious of quality, always exalting dilettantism as genius, and, above all, a shameful and embarrassing literary event. For this reason I have always remained an outside observer, sometimes frightened, sometimes shocked, sometimes indifferent, but always an outsider; I have been and still am an outside observer as much as I am an observer at all; what business do I have with literature, with your golden hair, Margarete, since the pen is my spade, the gravestone of your ashen hair, Julamith. Yes, this narrative, or let us say, novelette, is the monologue of a man, a rather young man still. This man whose parents gave him a strictly Christian upbringing, one could almost say strict to the point of bigotry, discovers in the days of the apocalypse that he, too, is marked by the broken seal: in the *spirit* of the so-called law that suddenly goes into effect, he qualifies to be a Jew. Then, before he is carted off to a ghetto, cattle train, who knows where, least of all he himself – he knows not what type of death penalty awaits him – he decides to write his story: "the story of decades of cowardice and self-denial," as he says, that is to say, as I have him say. What's most interesting in all this is that in his brand-new existence as a Jew he finds his escape from his Jew-complex and his salvation all at the same time. For what he has to recognize is the fact that by being excluded from one community one does not automatically become a member of another. "What do I have to do with Jews?" he asks, that is to say, I have him ask. Now that he, too, is one, he awakens, is awakened, to the recognition that he has nothing to do with them. While he was enjoying the privilege of non-Jewishness, he suffered on account of the Jews, the Jewish existence, or more precisely, on account of the corrupt, suffocating, murderous, and murder-inducing suicidal system of exclusions and discriminations. He suffered because of some of his friends, colleagues, his environs, which he believed to be his homeland; he suffered because of their hatred, limitations, fanaticism. He especially dreaded the unavoidable debates on anti-Semitism, the tortuous futility of all these debates, for as he realizes – I make him realize – anti-Semitism is not a conviction but a question of inclination and of moral character, it is "the ethics of despair, the mad rantings of self-haters, the vitality of the moribund," says he, that is to say, I have him say. On the other hand, there were some tensions in his relationship to Jews as well in that he tried to love them but was never sure that his attempts ever succeeded. There were some Jewish acquaintances, even friends, whom he liked and those whom he didn't. But this is something different, because he liked or disliked them for purely personal reasons. But how can one fundamentally like an abstract concept as, for example, Jewishness? How can one like an unknown mass stuffed into this abstract concept? If he succeeded, he only succeeded in liking them the way one likes an abandoned animal one has to take care of but doesn't know what it dreams about and what it is capable of. Now he had rid himself of this pain of his assumed responsibility. Now he can, in good conscience, reject those whom he rejects and he no longer has to like those he doesn't like. He is liberated because he no longer has a homeland. All that is left to decide now is the state of his death. Should he die as Jew, as Christian, as hero or as victim, perhaps even as a metaphysical absurdity, the victim of a neo-chaos of the demiurge? Since none of these concepts means anything to him, he decides not to taint the positive purity of his death by a lie. He sees everything in simple terms because he has earned the right of clairvoyance: "Let's not search for meaning where there is none: this century, this command squad, unceasingly executing orders is, once again, preparing for decimating, and it turns out that one of the tenths happened to be me. That's all." These were his last words, spoken by me, of course. Of course, all this is not quite so tense, but here I limited myself to the bare essentials; I am leaving out all of the dialogue, the turns of events, the setting, the other characters, and, further, his lover who deserts him. At the end we see our man sitting on the ground, shaken by uncontrollable laughter. This is what I intended the title to be: "The Laughter," but the editor at the press changed it. This editor is known by all to always carry a gun to work – to his office at the press – not the type clearly visible on uniformed police, not on a belt, but stuck in his bulging rear pocket; this editor discarded my title as "cynical" and "treading on the sanctity of memories," etc., etc.; still, even if under a mutilated title, the story did, indeed, appear in print, something I still don't understand and don't want to understand because it perhaps disgusts me to understand and discover the untangleable texture of hidden agendas that show no mercy, destroy everything, and whatever they allow to exist, only allow to exist with an intention to destroy. In this manner, then, like my fictive creation, I, too, will content myself by saying that in the process of the decimation (actually elimination by threes) somehow, who knows how, my story got dealt a lucky number. What struck my wife in this story was that *one can make a decision concerning one's Jewishness,* she said. Until now, she said, whenever she read a text about Jews or concerning Jews, she felt *as if her face were stuck in the mud*. Now, for the first time, said my wife, she felt that she could *lift up her face*. As a result of having read my story, my wife said, she felt the way my "hero" did, who, while he did die at the end, partook of an *internal liberation* first. Even if only for a period of time, she, too, experienced that liberating feeling, my wife said. That writing, my wife said, *taught her to live* more than anything else ever before, and as she spoke, for the second time that evening that smile moved across her face, that fast-changing undulating play of waves, that chromaticity of smiles, I can't call it any other name, that facial play that made me feel like melting away and becoming totally malleable. Soon I found out the background for her statements, her childhood and early adulthood. Even though my wife was born after Auschwitz, her childhood and young adulthood were spent in the shadow of Auschwitz. Or, to be more precise, marked by Jewishness, marked by mud, to quote my wife's earlier term. My wife's parents had been in Auschwitz; I knew her father, a tall, bold man, carefully acerbic among strangers, limitlessly self-abandoned and bitter in the circle of his close friends and family; she lost her mother when she was very young. Her mother died of some malady contracted at Auschwitz; at times she would bloat, then she would lose weight, then she had colic, then she was covered with spots. With her malady she posed an impossible task to science, just as a science found the source of her malady, Auschwitz, an impossibility too: for my wife's mother's malady was, in fact, Auschwitz, and one can never recover from Auschwitz, no one can ever recover from the Auschwitz malady. Incidentally, my wife did tell me that the determining factor in her becoming a doctor was her mother's illness and premature death. Later, as we were talking of these subjects, my wife quoted a sentence or two which she said she could never forget but which she could no longer remember where she read. I realized, not immediately, but soon thereafter, that my wife must have read these sentences in Nietzsche, namely in the volume *On the Utility and Harm of History,* and that again confirmed my conviction that those sentences we have a need for will, sooner or later, find us, because without this conviction I can't explain how these sentences could have reached my wife, who was never – to my knowledge at least – interested in philosophy, least of all in Nietzsche. These sentences, which I quickly looked up in my ancient red-bound Nietzsche volume, acquired once in a dark corner of an antiquarian shop and in the process of falling apart, read like this, not in my own but in Odon Wildner's fine translation: "There is a stage of sleeplessness, the surging of the past, a sense of history where actual reality is at a disadvantage and finally perishes, be it the individual's, nation's, or a whole culture's." Then, or perhaps just preceding, I can't remember right now, "whoever cannot settle down on the threshold of the moment, forgetting all that is past, whoever is incapable, fearlessly and without feeling dizzy, of planting his feet and hand firmly at a spot like the goddess of Victory," and from here on my wife knew it by heart: "that person will never know what happiness is and, what's worse, he will never be able to make another happy." My wife was made aware of her Jewishness and everything that went along with it at an early age. There was a period of her life – "the pony-tailed freckled little girl period," my wife said – when she imagined that *all other children must love her* on that account. Now, as I write down her words, I can suddenly see her, how she laughed as she spoke these words. Later on her Jewishness because synonymous with her sense of utter hopelessness: a sense of defeat, despondency, suspicion, hidden fears, her mother's sickness. A dark secret among strangers, a ghetto of Jewish feelings and Jewish thoughts at home. After the death of her mother her paternal aunt moved in with them. "She had such an Auschwitz face, I thought," said my wife; in every person she saw a former or a would-be murderer. "I don't understand how I grew up to be a relatively normal woman." Whenever Jewish matters were discussed she left the room. "Something turned to stone within me and resisted." She spent almost no time at home, studying was an escape, and later, so was medical school and her lovers, a few short, passionate affairs. She said she had "two horrifying experiences." She remembered both as happening when she was sixteen or seventeen. Once, all excited, she spoke of the French Revolution and said that that revolution was not that much better than the Nazis. Her aunt replied that she, as a Jew, cannot speak of the French Revolution this way because were it not for the French Revolution, Jews would still be living in ghettos. After having been corrected by her aunt this way, my wife remembered not having spoken a single word at home for days, perhaps even months. She felt she no longer existed, that she couldn't lay claim to any individual feelings or thoughts, and that she was merely entitled to *Jewish feelings* and *Jewish thoughts,* exclusively for the simple reason that she was born a Jew. That was the time when the phrase occurred to her and she first voiced it to herself: *they press her face in the mud on a daily basis*. Her other experience was this: she sat, book in hand, the book full of horrors and photographs of horrors, a spectacled face with a blank look behind barbed wires, a yellow-starred small boy with arms lifted, his gigantic cap sliding over his eyes, accompanied by two armed men – she was looking at those pictures, and some cold, malicious feeling was stirring in her heart, which frightened even her: she thought precisely the same thing as what my "hero" thought in my story. "What's that to me? After all, I, too, am a Jew," my wife said. But until she read these and other, similar thoughts in my story, she always thought of them with terror and always accompanied by a sense of guilt. That's why she felt, my wife said, that after reading my story *she was able to lift up her face*. And she repeated, more than once, that I was the one *teaching her to live,* that next to me she felt free. Yes, now in my dark and illuminating night these are the voices, pictures, motives that emerge from the texture of those few lightning-fast years that constituted my marriage, until, suddenly, I see us at the window of our flat – it was, again, night; not a winter but a spring night when some fragrance, like a message from another world, occasionally succeeds in piercing through the city's stench; perhaps the fragrance of plants from far away that, as if from habit, begin to awaken and, as if from habit, want to live again – when we saw three semidrunk men stumbling homeward from the bar nearby on the other side of the street. The white collar of the suede coat of one of them flashed up to our window; they sang holding on to each other; the last cars just hushed by, there was a moment's silence, and then, like at a choral interlude, their voices reached us loud and clear; we could hear well what they were singing: *We just returned from Auschwitz, there are more of us now than there were then,* their voices flowed in the night. At first I didn't really hear them, then I did, but what is it to me, I thought; that so-called anti-Semitism is such private affair of which I personally may die anywhere or anytime but still, today, after Auschwitz, I thought, this would be anachronistic; as H. would say, not H. Führer and Chancellor, but H. all Führers' and Chancellors' philosopher and chief wine steward, that worldview is no longer present; it would, therefore, be sheer provincialism, nothing more, *genius loci* – local idiocy, and if they wanted to shoot me or beat me to death, I thought, they would let me know, I thought, as they usually did so in the past. Then and only then did I look at my wife; cautiously, because she had been suspiciously quiet, and I could see in the cold light of the street and the warmer light streaming from our room behind us that tears were streaming down her face. There will never be an end to it, my wife said, no end to this curse, no escape; if only she knew what made her a Jew, she said, since she is incapable of believing in the religion for some reason, negligence, perhaps, or cowardice, or as the result of some personal preference or another, she simply doesn't know the specifically Jewish culture of the Jews and is incapable of being interested in finding out because she is simply not interested she said. What, then, makes her a Jew, she asked, when neither language nor lifestyle, nothing, nothing whatsoever, differentiates her from these others around her unless it is some secret ancient message hidden in her genes which she herself can't hear and therefore cannot know? And then, calmly, harshly, almost intentionally, like a well-aimed stab with the sword or a sudden hard embrace, I told her that all that was in vain, she looked for faulty reasons, false explanations in vain; the one singular fact that made her a Jew was this and nothing else: that she had *not* been to Auschwitz. My wife fell silent first like a scolded child, but then her face soon changed back into her own, the face of my wife, which was familiar to me, but also that of someone else whom I just discovered that instant in my wife's familiar face, so that I was shaken by the recognition. Thereafter our no-longer-all-that-passionate nights heated up again. Yes, by then, some of the contradictions of my marriage began to manifest themselves, or to be more precise, my marriage began to manifest what it was: a contradiction. As I remember those days I remember best some of my reflexes, which kept me in a constant state of tension and internal upheaval, the way, or so at least I imagine, instincts move beavers, those essentially ratlike little creatures, to build and rebuild their complicated systems of dams, caverns, corridors, even castles. At that time, the ideas for a longer work or novel occupied my mind, aside, of course, from my daily occupation: literary translation in pursuit of a living. The subject of the novel, incidentally, was to be the journey of a soul, the journey from darkness to light, the struggle for joy, the accomplishment of this task in victory: *happiness viewed as an obligation*. In those days, my wife and I spoke a great deal – nay, incessantly – of this plan. My wife visibly delighted in these conversations because of the idea of the novel in which – not entirely without grounds – she saw a monument to our marriage. Thus, she never had enough of my talking about it, painting it in broad strokes, sketching initially, then growing daily by detailed action, increasing, tightening, dividing motives, ideas to which, in the midst of the chromaticism of sudden illumination followed by calm flashes across her face, she too offered some timid comments, which in the hope for further facial chromatic display I approved, encouraged, and praised. We raised this plan together, so to say, cuddled, spoiled it like a baby. Looking at it retroactively, all this, undoubtedly, was a mistake; it was a mistake to allow my wife to enter this most sensitive, most secret, most vulnerable sphere of my existence, my *work* in one word, and which sphere, on the contrary, I must protect and defend as I have done ever since and as I have done before my marriage, surround it with barbed wire against all intruders, all intrusion, even against the potential of any intrusion. It is beyond doubt that I sensed the danger in my wife's intense, all-encompassing and permeating, vigorous and yet timidly tender interest; on the other hand, it's true, I didn't want to do without this interest as we don't want to do without the sudden burst of warm sunshine after the interminable, dark days of winter. As I commenced with the realization of the plan, that is to say, the writing of the novel, it turned out that the conception was impossible to carry out; it turned out that from my pen, as from some malignant growth, some substance kept seeping into the texture of the whole organism, its every cell, that mutated the texture and every one of its cells, so to say. It turned out that one – at least not I, which in this case amounts to the same thing – cannot write about happiness; happiness, perchance, is too simple a concept to enable one to write about, I wrote on a piece of paper then, which I am reading and copying over now. A life lived happily is a life lived mutely, I wrote. It turned out that to write about life means to think about life, to think about life is to question it, and the only one to question the element of his life is one suffocated by it or feeling out of place for one reason or another. It turns out, I don't write to find joy;

on the contrary, it turns out, I seek pain, the sharper the better, bordering on the unbearable sort, quite probably because pain is truth, and the answer to the question of what constitutes truth is quite simple, I wrote: truth is what consumes. All this, naturally, I did not share with my wife. On the other hand, I didn't want to lie to her either. In the course of our time spent together, in our conversations, we thus encountered certain difficulties, especially when the discussion turned to my work, more precisely, to the expectable results of my work; writing as *literature,* the notion of pleasing or not pleasing, a notion far removed, totally uninteresting to me, the question of the *meaning* of my work, questions mostly derailing into the filthy, shameful, humiliating, ridiculing thematic circle of success or lack of success. How could I have explained to my wife that my pen was my spade? That my only reason for writing was that I had to, and I had to because even then they whistled to me to dig deeper, to play death's tune darker, more sweetly? How could I complete my self-annihilation, my only business on earth, while nourishing some deceptive thought in the back of my mind, deceptive thoughts of *results, literature,* or even *success?* How could my wife, or, for that matter, anyone, wish me to *use* my self-liquidation as a spectacle, to use it to sneak in as a thief with his skeleton keys in some sort of literary or other future from which I was excluded by way of my birth and from which I, too, excluded myself? How could I be expected to perform work predicated on this future using the very same spade with which I must dig my grave into the clouds, the wind, into nothing? The question was, did I see my situation this clearly, this unequivocally, then as I write it down now? Probably not, but it was not for lack of intention or effort. What I must have been thinking in those days, and the emotions with which I was struggling, is well demonstrated by a fragmentary piece I found in looking through the fragments of my marriage. It's obvious that this piece of paper was initially intended to go next to my wife's teacup, as was my custom at times when on account of my *work* reaching well into the night I didn't get up for breakfast. It said: "so that we may love each other and yet remain *free,* even though I know quite well that neither one of us can escape the male or female fate which was assigned to us by some secret and, admittedly, not particularly wise nature; that is to say, that it will happen again that I'll reach out for you and wish, wish nothing but to make you mine, and at the same time when you, too, reach out for me and are finally mine, I will still put limits on your self-giving to preserve that which I believe to be *my freedom.*" That's it for the fragment, and since it got mixed in with my writing, it is certain that I didn't lean it against my wife's teacup but left it somehow with my notebooks; but it is also certain that this is the way I thought and lived accordingly, nay, lived my thoughts, since *I have always had a secret life* and that *has always been the real one.* Yes, those were the days I began building my hidden corridors, beaver dam fortifications to hide and protect them from my wife's sight and hands, so that occasionally and undoubtedly because of my protective gates, I sensed some latent resentment in my wife's behavior, this perception in turn became first a resentment on my part and then a lasting pain which made – wanted to make – my wife's temporary annoyance appear a much worse resentment than it really was; after all, it wouldn't have taken that much to mollify my wife, one single, precise, well-chosen word, or perhaps even a single gesture would have done it, but I was rather fond of my pain. I was obviously fond of my pain because I recognized my castaway nature in it, the unbearable feeling of being a castaway, in turn, urged me to compensate, this lonely compensation then assumed the form of inspiration in me; that is to say, it ignited my neurosis anew, my all-sweeping all-superseding desire to work, which forced me to invent ever new defense reflexes. If ignited, this work-fever, work-madness, in one word, the whole devilish mechanism, that murderous carousel which first dips me in pain and then leaves me high above it, but only and exclusively to throw me back even deeper . . . and certainly, quite certainly this, too, played a role in reigniting the passion of our nights. On one of these dark shimmering nights whose dark, velvety blackness greatly differed from the dark black lights of my nights today, on one of these ignited dark nights, then, my wife said we could only respond to all our questions and answers, these questions and answers touching the very core of our lives with the core of our lives, or more precisely, with our total lives, because all further questions and all further answers would be unsatisfactory otherwise and that she, for one, could only imagine her wholeness one way; no other wholeness could substitute for the one and only, total, unsurpassable, *true* wholeness, said my wife – in other words, she wanted my child, yes, indeed, and

"No!" I said immediately and forthwith, without hesitation and spontaneously, so to say, for it is quite obvious that our instincts actually work against our instincts, so that, so to say, our anti-instincts act instead of or even for our instincts; and either that this

"No!" was not a decisive enough

"No!" or an expected response, given my unpredictability, and my wife only laughed at me. She does understand me, she said later, she knows from how deep inside this "No!" sprang, and how much I have to struggle and conquer within me in order to make it a "*Yes*." And I answered her, I believed I understood her and knew what she was thinking but that the

"No!" was a

"No!" Not some sort of *Jewish "no,"* which she probably had in mind, no, I was quite certain of this, as certain as I was uncertain as to the nature of the

"No!" only that it was a

"No!" I said, even though, as concerns Jewishness, there would be plenty of reasons, for I could imagine a desperate and wretched conversation, I said. For instance, imagine the child's, our child's – or your – explosion if, let's say, the child hears something and starts screaming, "I don't want to be a Jew!" because it is quite imaginable and certainly warranted, I said, that, let's say, the child wouldn't want to be a Jew, and I said it would not be easy to answer for that, because how could one force a living being to be a Jew? In that respect, I said, I would have to walk with lowered head before the child – and you – because I couldn't give the child – or you – anything: no explanation, no faith, no ammunition, for my Jewishness means nothing to me or, more precisely, it means nothing as Jewishness, abstractly speaking; as experience it means everything, as Jewishness it means: a bald woman in red robe in front of the mirror; as experience it means my life or rather my survival, a spiritual form of existence which I live and which I maintain and which suffices for me; I am perfectly content with this much; the question is, though, whether or not he/she/you would be content with it. And still, I said, I am not speaking of a Jewish "no," in spite of it all I am not, for there is nothing more awful, disgusting, destructive, and self-denying than this so-called rational "*no,*" this Jewish "no"; there is nothing cheaper, more cowardly than this, I said; I have had enough of seeing that murderers and life-deniers declare themselves publicly in favor of life; it happens too often, I said, to rouse even some sort of resentment in me; there is nothing more terrible, shameful than to deny life to please those who deny life; after all, children were born even in Auschwitz, I said, and my wife, for obvious reasons, liked my train of argument, although I don't believe she understood me just as I probably didn't understand myself. Yes, and shortly thereafter I had to board a streetcar, I was going somewhere, who knows where, presumably to go about my business – as if I had any business left since all my earthly business had long since been conducted – I was staring out of the window at the fall-like sensation of whizzing by and the unexpected intervals of stops. We sped noisily amid intimidating buildings and the thin strips of anemic vegetation here and there, when suddenly, like a daring coup, a family boarded the streetcar. I forgot to mention that it was Sunday, a discreetly dying Sunday afternoon in the warming-up season. There were the five of them, the parents and three girls, the youngest barely out of diapers; in pink, blue, and blond, she dazzled the eye. Her saliva running, she screamed determinedly. She must be warm, I thought. Her brown-haired, gentle, worn-out mother took her into her lap, her slender neck folded over the head of the child with the broken-arch movement of a ballerina. The middle girl stood skulking next to her mother, who was cuddling the baby, and the oldest girl, she must have been seven or eight, I thought, put her arm around her little sister in a gesture of reconciliation, one expressing the miserable solidarity of the excluded. The middle sister, though, shook it off angrily. She wanted to possess her mother, but she knew it was a lost cause since the tools of possession, uninhibited screaming, have now become the prerogative of the youngest child. The oldest girl remained alone, once again, to experience the bitterness of marginality, loneliness, and jealousy on this beautifully lit Sunday afternoon. Will this feeling mature into accepting forgiveness in her, I wondered, or into a neurosis to hide in a hole while her father and mother break her spirit into some shameful existence, I wondered, which she will put up with and which, embarrassedly, she will fulfill, and if not embarrassedly, then it's all the more shameful for her and all those who broke her spirit and accepted her lot, I was thinking. The father, a brown, sinewy man with glasses, in his Sunday pants and with sandals on his naked feet, boasted an Adam's apple like a growth; he extended his long, yellow hand and between his sharp knees the baby finally quieted down. On the five faces, like a transcendental message, a similarity beyond all their particulars suddenly emerged. They were all ugly, worn out, miserable, and glorified; a mixture of feelings waged war within me: disgust, attraction, horrifying memories, and melancholy; I saw it written on their foreheads, so to say, and in fiery letters written on the walls of the streetcar:

"No" – I could never be another person's father, fate, god,

"No" – It should never it happen to another child, what happened to me: my childhood,

"No" – something screamed and howled within me, it is impossible that this, this childhood, should happen to the child – to you – and to me. Yes, and that was the time when I started to tell my wife about my childhood, or, perhaps, it was myself, I don't really know, but I was telling her with all the generosity of my logorrhea, with all its compulsiveness, I was telling it uninhibited, for days and for weeks I continued telling it, actually even now, even though I'm no longer telling it to my wife. Yes, indeed, and it was not only telling that I started to do in those days but also wondering; this same city where I moved with the relative security of relative familiarity begun to turn into a trap in those days, and, at times, the city opened up under my feet so that I never knew in which unspeakable scene, saturated with tortures and outrage, I would unexpectedly find myself, what call I'd follow, for instance, when I snuck about among side streets napping like noble patients between the small, disabled, dreamwrecked palaces, hiding in the shadows of fairy-tale houses with turrets, wind vanes, lacy, steep-angled, blind-windowed facades along the black fences of wretched front yards where everything was so plundered, so bare, visible, worn, and rational, like an abandoned excavation site. Or, how on earth did I end up in the intestines, so to say, of this city whose inhabitant I happened to become anew either as an act of fate, if you like, or as a result of clumsiness, if you prefer. Let's call it an act of fate, if it's all the same anyway and since we may recognize our fates even in our own clumsiness, provided we have the eyes for it. Yes, indeed, in those days I believed, or rather I deceived myself with the belief perhaps, that I ended up here arbitrarily, without a purpose, here, in the same place, in the intestines of a city district called Jozsefvaros, where this district meets with the outskirts of a district called Ferencvaros, where, in other words, I still reside, albeit the prefab apartment of a prefab building was only a wretched plan on a wretched construction map in those days.

It was a late summer dusk, I remember, the city bathed in overripe smells, along the pathway drunk, irregular, small-windowed, unwashed houses staggered, the setting sun dripping down their walls like a sticky, yellow flow of pus; their gates were like darkly gaping wounds, and I dizzily grabbed a door handle or who knows what as I was suddenly touched – oh, not by the mystery of death, no, contrarily, by the mystery of survival. Yes, a murderer must feel this way, I thought and told my wife later. As to why I was thinking these thoughts, I believe while not logical it was still comprehensible; I must have been thinking them because of the dead, I told my wife, my dead, my dead childhood, my *impossible* unphantomable – at least in the context of my dead and my dead childhood – survival, yes, a murderer must feel this way, who, let's say, I thought and told my wife thereafter, had long forgotten his crime, which is quite possible and not that rare an occurrence, and, after decades, perhaps out of forgetfulness, or out of a mechanical repetition of his habitual behavior, suddenly opens the door to the scene of his crime and finds everything unchanged there: the corpse, having turned to a dusty skeleton, the cheap furniture, and also himself, and it doesn't matter that it's all obvious – nothing and no one is the same, but it is also perfectly obvious that after the short interval of a generation, everything is still the same, only more intensely so. And now he recognizes what he has to recognize, that it was *not* chance, *not in the least,* that led him back, what's more, it's possible that he never left the place because this is the place where he must do penance. And don't ask me, I told my wife, why he must, for sin and penance are concepts that are only connected by existence: that is, if existence does indeed create a connection; of course, if it does so, then existence by itself is sufficient for sin, *el delito mayor del hombre es haber nacido,* as has been written, I told my wife. I also told her about a dream of mine, a recurring, old dream which I hadn't dreamed in a long while but which started returning suddenly in those days. It always happens *there,* yes, *there,* always *there* on the same spot, in that corner building. I don't see the surroundings, but I know them for sure. Perhaps it is the walls that let me figure it out, the ghostly gray thick walls of an ancient building. And also the tobacco shop, which some ugly steep steps lead to. Upstairs, it is as if one opened the door to a rat hole: stuffy twilight and the breath of corpses. The tobacco shop, though, had been moved, farther up, to the corner of the building. There is absolutely no reason for me to open the door. I open it. This is not a tobacco shop, it's a little more spacious, a little lighter, much drier and warm like an attic. There they sit, opposite an indeterminable (perhaps an attic skylight) source of light from above dancing in the thick dust, on an ancient sofa placed on the concrete floor. All indications are that they just sat up, that they have been lying down waiting for my eventual visit for decades, waiting for the visit of the I-don't-care, hope-murdering grandchild. Two old people in the dusty light, full of reproaches. They are so weak they can barely move. I hand them the ham I brought along. They are glad, but glad with continued resentment. They speak but I don't understand. My grandfather's gray unshaven face is bent over the ham in his hands; he already opened the paper. On my grandmother's face the death spots are quite visible. She complains about constant headaches and noises in her ear. Also about the wait, the long, long wait. I clearly see how little the ham I brought for them is. They are incredibly hungry and neglected. I make a few futile gestures like a student trying to explain himself. My heart is heavy, like the stones of the stairs. Then everything disappears, flies away, dissipates like a shameful secret. Why do we always have to live facing some sort of shame? I noted down in those days. Also, at the same time the collection of ideas originated, one that, even today, keeps growing and is sitting here somewhere among the pieces of paper on my desk: a bunch of papers held together by a holder. *Friends, young adulthood was a harsh assignment for us; we suffered on account of our youth, as of a serious illness,* I'm reading on one of the notes. *Families, I hate you,* I read on another. *We delivered ourselves unto youth as unto death; I often pondered in my youth,* I read, *that the concept of rule is invariably one of terror,* then I read my comments attached to those of Thomas Bernhard: *"rule by terror, invariably means rule by the father."* Then all I read on the notes are personal observations such as: "The duty of education, which I could never reconcile . . ." "To affect someone else's dreams like a nightmare, to play a paternal, that is to say *final, decisive* role, is one of the genuine horrors, one of whose awful aspects is . . ." "That (in my childhood, and therefore ever since) everything that meant affirming myself has been considered sinful and everything virtuous if I acted denying or killing myself . . ." My grandmother's mouth never smelled good. Really, her breath smelled like moth flakes. The smell of the Josefvaros flat. The anachronistic breath of the Austro-Hungarian monarchy. The darkness of the flat, like that of the epoch, is the darkness of the thirties, an inherited darkness turned malady. The dark furniture, the building with corridors, the lives lived in front of others, the milky coffee for dinner, the matzos crumbled in the mug, the prohibition to turn on the lights, my grandfather, as he reads his newspaper in the dark, the alcove in whose mysterious corners a dark, musty, murderous thought seems to hide constantly. The nightly routine of killing bedbugs: "Gradually, I would surround you with all these stories, which are actually none of your business, but which, after a while, would tower around you like an insurmountable obstacle . . ." "And what an incredible misery childhood was and how impatiently I tried to grow up because I firmly believed in the secret community of grown-ups and that in their sadism-saturated world they lived in total security . . ." etc., etc. The mornings, rainy Monday mornings when my father was taking me to my boarding school for yet another week. Every Monday morning lives on as a rainy Monday morning in my memory, which, of course, is quite impossible, but quite typical, I told my wife. I recall that on just such a rainy Monday morning I suddenly got up, leaving everything, leaving my *work* aside, and started for that residential district, or more precisely, for that district that used to be a single-home residential neighborhood and which I remembered as such, as the turreted, wind-vaned, steep-roofed, gingerbread dreamhouse district where my boarding school used to stand as one of these turreted, wind-vaned, steep-roofed, gingerbread dreamhouses. Closing my umbrella, the shining example of our mortal grotesques, a slightly balding, reasonably established-looking fellow, must have entered this house of my confused terror and even more confused joy, wearing a checkered cap and carrying a dripping umbrella, I told my wife that evening. Is this triumph? Or is it defeat? How would I have received this fellow in the past? I remarked to my wife. Would I have noticed him at all, and if so, would I have thought him some sort of inspector, the accomplice of the administration, the powers that be, I told my wife that night. Or perhaps I would have thought him an annoying violin instructor. I presume I would have immediately noticed the fellow's clumsiness as well, something quite ridiculous that catches the eye right away: for instance, the way he spoke with the kids, so deliberately, articulately, like a lust-murderer, I told my wife. There is nothing, absolutely nothing about this fellow that resembles my fantasies concerning my adulthood, he cuts a strange, messed-up figure; at most I would have envied his sovereignty, not suspecting how much it is merely an adult sovereignty, that is to say, nonsovereignty appearing to be sovereignty, I told my wife. I jotted down a few lines about the visit in my old notepad; I shall copy a few of them down here. "I've been to the boarding school," I wrote, "it is all in ruins, like everything else, buildings, lives, the world." There was a commemorative plaque on the wall that surprised me a great deal. It said: *Here lived and worked,* etc., etc., our director. The boss. The Diri (as we, kids, called him. Who would have believed that he was a scholar? Yes, general dilettantism goes by the name of scholarship these days . . .). The grounds were in shambles, all dug up. The school converted to a tenement building. The festive staircase with its massive stone railing that was so wonderful to slide down on and where so many mysterious events took place, especially in the evenings when one trotted upstairs to go to bed, pushing and shoving among one's fellows, when sleepiness descended on one's eyes like freshly fallen snow, building, suppressing, quietly all round, experience and desire (when one night, suddenly, I was struck by high fever and chills, a peasant boy some ten years my senior carried me upstairs in his arms and asked me in which room I resided, and I couldn't respond because at five I have never heard of the word "reside" and, thus, didn't know its meaning). This staircase, then, well, let it suffice to say that it was filthy . . . The row of bedrooms, all chopped up, became apartments upon apartments . . . The Diri's residence . . . that frightening, quiet, and quieting apartment that forced one to tiptoe! On its door, a gray aluminum doorknob instead of the shining brass, like a victorious kick in the butt. The study rooms in the mezzanine. Once the second-ranked juniors and the much-envied seniors were bending over their books here during the afternoon hours of the *silentium*. The teacher constantly watching for appropriate awe. The occasionally respect-inspiring, difficult esoteric problem of an algebra assignment. These rooms now provide homes for several families. Noisy, busy, family lives filled with food smells . . . the dissipation of all strict form, its rotting. Mediocrity, the common, works like a dissolving force, like death, in the final analysis . . . The *suterain,* the dining hall; the *carcer,* the playroom (Ping-Pong). And most of all, the scene of the reports. One can't enter. The sign says *Film Club,* tickets, etc. Well, fine, I'll just imagine the dining hall; it's better this way anyway, then the so-called *reality* won't intrude (their reality, that is), high-set windows illuminated the parallel rows of long tables set with white cloth in that gigantic dining hall. The breakfast! The only worthy ceremony of the day (except for the Saturday reports), strict, yet dreamy. At my assigned place, the breakfast setting, my napkin signed with the Roman numeral one in my napkin ring also adorned with the Roman numeral one. Here that was my number, as, at other times, in other places, I acquired other numbers (today, for instance, there is an eleven-digit number floating about in my stead somewhere, in the nooks and crannies of unknown labyrinths, like my shadow-existence, my other, secret self, of which I know nothing even though I vouch for it with my life and whatever it does or whatever is done to it becomes my death penalty). But this Roman numeral one was indeed a classy beginning, pretty and promising like the dawn of culture. This was because I was the youngest inhabitant of the boarding school . . . etc. We stood at our places, all cleaned up, shiny, awake, and hungry. (I was always hungry, always.) At the head of the table stood a teacher; a teacher at the head of each table. He muttered a prayer. A short, cautious, one could say, diplomatic prayer. One had to be careful not to make it part of the canon, Jewish or Christian, that is to say, to make it both Jewish and Christian at the uniform pleasure of any Good. *"Give us this day, Lord, our daily bread,"* we said, I think, I'm not sure, but it was something like this. (In the evening, on the other hand, I prayed in German: *Müde bin ich, geh zu Ruh* . . . etc.) I didn't understand a single word of it but learned it quickly and with it the reassuring monotony of prayer, the urge of repetition; I practiced this very particular form of hygiene, the potential omission of which would have caused a more severe wound in my soul than, for instance, the omission of brushing my teeth . . . I remembered my childhood's strong, imposed religiosity, which, initially, was essentially animistic, later accompanied by an all-seeing invisible X-ray vision . . . but that only came, if I remember correctly, after my father took over my *education* . . . mostly, anyway. Further on, the *carcer:* a dark, bug-infested storage room. Once they locked me up. I viewed it rationally: from the point of view of the love of solitude, the love of illness. The phantasmagorism of fever. Early decadence. Or, perhaps, simply well-justified misanthropy? To lounge about half-asleep and all alone in the large dormitory, to watch the sun reach the top of chestnut trees in the garden, while a cat with its incomparable gait undulating the tip of its tail snuck all the way across the rooftop opposite the window, a rooftop full of incredible adventures, hidden nooks and crannies, chimneys and turrets. The sudden cramp in my stomach in the evening when the inevitable was about to occur, on account of which my stomach was queasy all afternoon: steps on the staircase, then loud, earth-shattering steps in the corridor. The others. *They are coming,* I whispered to myself, deathly pale, like news of a catastrophe. At any rate – cramps in the stomach. It started with the extra helping of milk in the morning . . . on account of my anemia. (The marvelous pleasure of the old milk bottles that, as it turned out, were just as fragile and fleeting as the pearls of dew on these new slender glasses whose surfaces are mildly rough to the touch and are covered by alternating flat and sharp vertical surfaces.) I had to drink it down. Then, for a long time, my stomach hurt. I bent over like after a KO . . . When they locked me in the *carcer,* self-pity finally got the better of me. It came in handy because I knew I had to put on a sad face when the key was turned, and they came to let me out so that they would enjoy the assumed misery they doled out for me. (I knew of these little subterfuges, spontaneously, from an inborn insidiousness, or, perhaps they weren't inborn, only acquired very early – did my *successful* education, therefore, *bear fruit?*) . . . By then I have long recognized what a disgusting place this world was for a small child (what I did not realize was the fact that this was not going to change unless I did) . . .

I recall the headaches. I can't help remembering the headaches. Migraines, to be exact. That's what they were. I couldn't move my head; it ached from the light passing through my eyes. I didn't dare to mention it to anyone, ever. I didn't think they'd believe me, they could believe it was believable. I thought this, too, was my secret – and therefore bound to be kept secret – sin, like the other things, like everything. At the end, I didn't believe my head when it hurt. Here, too, we see the success of my education . . . One needs to ponder the survivability of the whole thing, the period of my life between five and ten years. It is almost inconceivable: how did I do it? Obviously, just like the others, like everyone else: with the help of severe inflictions of irrationality to my rationality. With the help of insanity, with the help of a servant's insanity, different from (or perhaps, contrarily, identical with) the master's insanity.

The first concrete instance of insanity was the divorce of my parents, which was made especially significant because of its consequence, namely, the boarding school. When I kept asking them as to the reasons for their divorce, I always got the same answer: *We didn't understand each other,* they both said. How come? After all, they both spoke Hungarian, I thought. I simply couldn't comprehend why they didn't understand what they understood. But this was the final word, the ultimate argument, the border demarcating a void beyond: I thus suspected some grave, complex, and presumably dirty secret behind it, one that was forced upon me. It was like a death sentence, I had to accept it, all the more so because I didn't understand it. The other point of demarcation for irrationality was some regular trips on the tram with my father. I no longer recall where we were going, to whom, or why. The whole affair was much less significant than the divorce. But still . . . I remember the stop where we always got off and then we had to walk a long way. I mentioned that if we continued on the tram and got off at the next station, we would only have to walk a few steps back. My father answered: *I am not going to walk back.* Question: *Why not?* Answer: *Because I am not going to walk back.* New Question: *But why not?* New Answer: *I told you, because I am not going to go back*. I sensed the profound depth of this recalcitrance but could not make heads or tails out of it. With the total puzzlement of my intellect I was facing some sort of alluded-to secret. In the end, I had to assume the presence of some inscrutable but unassailable law which my father represented and recognize the power being wielded over me. Neurosis and force, the only forms of interaction; adopting, the only possible means of survival; doubting, an exercise; madness, the end result, I wrote down. *An earlier culture turns to ruins, then, finally, to ashes, but above the ashes spirits still hover* (Wittgenstein), I found on one of my pieces of paper, and also . . . as I stood there, under my umbrella, and as I was touched by the suffocating secrets of this institution, this well-to-do private establishment, this former *boys' boarding school,* secrets that even today surround it in the damp, fall air, just as muteness always hovers around graves to be dug, then, suddenly, it dawned on me, it struck me through and through, so to say, to the bone like this penetrating dampness . . . this *is* the *earlier culture,* this father-culture, this universal father-complex, I noted. Later on, as I was reading, I thought I recognized "my institute" in the descriptions of jails, seminaries, military schools, but, of course, my school was still different, kinder, more absurd, and, on the whole, more perverse, albeit I only recognized this for sure after many years in the mirror of all-accomplishing depravity, I told my wife. The institute simply copied the ideas of the outside world, and viewed these ideas, out of habit, or comic mistake, or habit turned comic misunderstanding, as the trademark of rule, I told my wife. The walls of all study rooms were decorated by the portraits of all Hungarian father-usurpers: between royal and imperial majesties and chief and first ministers there was the bust of a man respectfully titled His Most Honorable Highness the Governor, dressed in a hat as large as the sea and a mysterious, fringed uniform, I told my wife. Thus, I told my wife, I retroactively had the suspicion that the running of the institute may have been influenced by concepts of Anglo-Saxon leadership, of Anglo-Saxon *education* with some elements of Austrian-German, no, Austro-Hungarian, no, German-Austro-Hungarian-minority-Jewish assimilation, on account of the *genius loci*. And, I continued to tell my wife, there was, of course, the difference of substituting members of the mid or low or lower Budapest bourgeoisie for the elite of world empires to be trained. Spartan principles, I told my wife, manifested themselves mostly in the lack of sufficient food: food was stolen from the children by the learned members of the administration and faculty, influenced by the ideals of Anglo-Saxon education, probably, again, on account of the *genius loci*. I also told my wife about the commemorative plaque. How surprised I was to see it. Undoubtedly, I told my wife, I could, if I wanted to, find out more about it, the commemorative plaque I mean, about the reasons for it, etc., but that, as far as I was concerned, I didn't wish to know anything. It is a fact: this man, the director and, at the same time, proprietor of our institute, was surrounded by an aura of immense authority; this authority, however, had nothing whatsoever to do with the respect due to higher and noble things. As is generally the case with authority, his, too, was based on well-organized fear, I told my wife. Even though he was a rather ridiculous figure (I mentioned the nickname we children gave him: *the Plug*): a small, little man, compact, with a yellowish-white mustache, a long bohemian mane of flowing white hair; his stomach, like an independent member, protruding like a ripe watermelon from under his gray vest. Incidentally, I told my wife, our fear was occasioned neither by deeds of brutality nor some mean words. But fear, my dear, I told my wife, works on transpositions, and when it solidifies into world order is precisely when it is usually no more than superstition. The teachers were afraid of him, or, at least, they acted as if they were. He served as a constant reference, his approach was accompanied by whispers, hushes, and general consternation. The Diri! The Diri is coming! But he only came rarely. From his apartment on the second floor, as from a castle in the clouds, his orders descended; in fact, often they weren't even expressed wishes but wishes attributed to him or, one could say, anticipated of him. We lived in the shadow of the cloud-castle, always looking up to its heights, observing the castle, but with faces shadowed by it. A seriousness ruled, the well-founded reasons for which no one doubted, a kind of suffocating but at the same time officially gay-masked seriousness. The spirit of playing by the rules, the spirit of sportsmanship, the approaching exams of the seniors, the spirit of their graduation. The spirit of modernity. Full, though, of classical traditions. And full, too, of national intent, national poems, national mourning, national struggles. I remember the legends, I told my wife, those that circulated among us about the meals taken upstairs to the cloud-castle from the kitchen in the souterrain via the back steps: there was always someone who happened to see what was taken upstairs for lunch or dinner for the Diri and his family, while we were chewing on four pieces of sausage in a watery potato stew or munched on the five pieces of dry biscuit served with our evening tea. But privilege, my dear, I told my wife, only solidifies authority and the hatred mingled with admiration with which we, the disenfranchised, viewed these demonstrations suited the generally perceived dualities of our lives. Although, I told my wife, the seriousness occasionally collapsed with a great sound of breaking and splitting and fell into an abyss lined with obscene sounds of laughter, from where the insane shouts of resident demons emanated but from where, although admittedly shook up like a battleship lifted from the depths of the sea but which, even then, as a wreck retains its glorious majesty, the old authority, the castle in the clouds, order reemerged again and again. Scandal, I told my wife, scandal was the term they used to describe these inevitable, always unexpected, and, one could say, rain falls. You must imagine these, I told my wife, in the manner of when a drunk gentleman, after controlling himself for a while, finally gives in to temptation and falls down with a sigh, relaxing; yes, indeed, missteps here were just the same, except that as concerns the gentleman of the analogy, his sobriety is nothing but a misstep too, a loss of ground under his feet, only that his sobriety is a drunkenness to the *n*th degree. I told my wife about one of these scandals. One that was most characteristic. It happened when "Pudge," a stocky, aging, heavy-handed educator, stormed through the dormitories one morning and discovered that someone was missing: a senior, a seventeen-year-old boy; I still remember his white teeth, his expressive face, his long brown hair, and his laughter, I told my wife. At the same time (but it's possible it happened earlier), he also discovered that the little room at the end of the hallway wouldn't open, that is to say, that it was locked and that it was locked from the inside. At the same time (but it's possible it was earlier), it was reported from the kitchen that the "new girl" was missing. I remember the girl, too, as she served the tables in her apron, although, actually, all I really recall are thick blond curls and a rather typical, I could say archetypal, smile. Supposedly they locked themselves in in the evening and then fell asleep. "Pudge" now hammered at the door. There were some hesitant movements, some subdued whispers, and then there was no noise whatsoever from within. They didn't open the door. "Pudge" called upon the sinners by name. Before long the Diri arrived. His face scarlet, his mustache and hair flowing, his stomach jumping up and down – we, the subversive underlings opened up a path for him to walk through as we pressed against the wall. He pulled on the doorknob like the Gestapo, he beat the door with his two fists like a cuckolded husband in a cheap vaudeville play. Then all I remember is the boy's public expulsion (the girl was kicked out immediately); I remember the pretentious, sanctimonious, hypocritical text and the fact that we all took the senior's side, and also that we all remained silent. Naturally, you would say, I told my wife. Today I know the reasons for my sense of sin, guilt, fear, and shame then, that suffocating something that I felt through the whole procedure; today I know what sort of a ritual I witnessed then in the father-substitutional paternalistic institute: I witnessed a *public castration,* which happened for the sake of our intimidation and *with our cooperation,* that is to say, they castrated our pal with our cooperation in order to *intimidate us;* in other words, they made us the ultimately perverse participants of an ultimately perverse act, I told my wife, and it is totally irrelevant whether they did this knowingly or simply out of habit, simply out of educational habit, the destroying habit of destructive education. Or, take for instance, the ritual of the afternoon *rapports* every Saturday, I told my wife. She must picture these, too, I told her. First they would bring the long tables from the dining room so as to make a single, endlessly long table, then they covered them with tablecloths. All this took place in the game room. At this point we, the inmates, arrived so as to line up across from this endlessly long empty row of tables and the row of chairs beside it. Nervousness began to descend upon us in an almost tangible way. Then someone, usually a lower-ranked teacher, but occasionally a higher-ranked member of a lower ranked class of employees, brought in a large book bound in black, the *rapport-book,* and, without saying a word, he placed it on the table. Another wait followed, black silence ominously spreading on the chairs and the white table, a wait of little hope vis-à-vis the mean, flat *rapport-book.* At that moment, the moment of general consternation, sighs, yes, the moment of total breakdown, the Diri entered at the head of the faculty. They sat down. There was deathly silence. The noise of eyeglasses being adjusted. Some clearing of throats, creaking of chairs. Then, when the tension could no longer be increased, the black book was opened, just like the book of the Apocalypse. Everyone was listed in there, everyone's every sin (and virtue). Each one of us was called upon by name. The person called upon stepped forward and walked trembling and lonely across the space between the enthroned majesties behind the table and the warmth of the flock behind. Weighing his accomplishments, his omissions with some certainty, yet growing more and more insecure, he would stand there prepared for any surprise. The Diri read the weekly entries concerning the boy quietly, turned to the left, turned to the right, whispering with the teachers who turned their mouths or their ears to him, whichever was called on, then the verdict was spoken. This could take the form of chiding, praise, upgrading; the boy could be held up as an example to all others, or he could be deprived of his Saturday or even his Sunday leave. But this was unimportant, I told my wife; what really mattered, what only mattered was the act itself, the procedure. I felt perhaps I shouldn't be telling her all these things, at least not in this way, talking about them constantly for days and weeks because I could possibly be boring her and definitely torturing her with this as, much later, though, I tortured her. But I tortured myself as well, to be more precise, I tortured myself not less but also differently, more creatively, so to say. I felt this already as I was telling my wife about my childhood; even then I felt during my speech how the ancient boil of my childhood was incessantly collecting, growing, ripening – perhaps reinfected because of the new danger – wanting to burst open and, indeed, bursting open . . . Thus while I did torture myself with my speech, I was also relieved by the speech and the torture. This act of the Saturday *rapports*, this procedure, I told my wife, was like divine judgment as imagined, let's say, by a chaplain; this act was like the *Appel* at Auschwitz, I told her, not yet real, of course, only in jest. Later I discovered that the Diri, too, went up in smoke in one of those crematoriums, and if I am to take this fact as his final, ultimate confirmation, then I must quite possibly take this to be the fruit of the successful education I received at his hands, of the *culture* in which he believed and for which he prepared us pedagogically.

From this actually still detached and rather impersonal and therefore unpredictable world of pedagogical dictatorship, I ended up suddenly at the age of ten under a paternal, warmhearted tyranny, because my father decided to take over my education, I told my wife. At this time, I remember, I tried several times to put to paper my feelings about and toward my father; my father's and my – how shall I say it – rather complicated relationship, or to create an at least somewhat exact portrait of him, even if I was not doing him justice, for how can we do justice when it concerns our fathers, how can we do justice even when it concerns truth itself, since for me only one truth exists, *my truth,* even if it is a delusion, yes, my delusion; my delusion – good God! – can only be validated by my life, as truth . . . I tried, then, to create at least an acceptable portrait of my father and of my feelings toward him, of my relationship to him. But I never succeeded, and today I understand that it was doomed never to succeed, and I have a suspicion, a hunch, that I have continued to try ever since, and that in the final analysis that's all I am doing now and am now, as ever, trying in vain. "I must be able to recognize how impossible it was for him to find the path leading to me . . ." I wrote down, for instance. "Quite probably he was bound to me, as to himself, by an uneasy emotion which he quite probably called love and took for love and which indeed was love if we accept this word in its impotence and disregard its tyrannical contents . . . ," I wrote. At the boarding school I had to deal with laws which, while I feared them, I never respected, I told my wife. Actually, it resembled fate in the sense that it could strike me down or it could favor me but never in any circumstance touch my conscience; I only became a genuine sinner under the yoke of love, I told my wife. This segment of my childhood threw me into a crisis; I existed in an animistic spiritual setting. Like the caveman is, so my thoughts were fenced in by so many taboos that I almost attributed material strength to them; I believed in their omnipotence, I told my wife. At the same time, however, undoubtedly under my father's influence, I suspected an Almighty One who knows my every thought at conception and weighs them . . . and in those days I was often besieged by unweighable thoughts. It was my father's habit, I told my wife, to give me an occasional lecture. On such occasions it was impossible for him to avoid repetition. *That is to say,* I told my wife, I always knew what he was about to say, so that secretly I was always ahead of him in the text as in some sort of recital, and he continued to repeat to me obediently. For a moment I regained my freedom, but it made my skin break out in goose bumps, I told my wife. Petrified, I tried to hold on to anything: it sufficed to notice his awkward crumpled collar, the loneliness of his slightly trembling hand, the concentration of the knitting of his brow, his whole futile misery – anything that would finally soften me and from which, like a desiccated sponge, I would turn to dust. Then I could finally utter inwardly the words of my salvation: *Poor man . . .* Then the sponge began to swell, my own pity moved me to tears, and this is how I paid my installments on the debt constantly weighing upon me through my father's threatening love. Now whether, in spite of all and above all, I did still love him in all the ambiguities of our sense of the word, I answered my wife when she asked me, I do not know and it would be extremely difficult for me to know, because faced with so many demands, so many resentments, I have always known, felt, and perceived that I don't love him or at least don't love him sufficiently, and since I didn't know how to love him, I consequently probably didn't, I told my wife. And, I told my wife, it seems to me that this is the way things are, expressing myself perhaps a little radically, this is the way it was meant to be, because this way and only this way can we establish an abstract schemata of existence. Power is unquestionable; its laws are unquestionable, according to which we must live but we can never totally satisfy the laws: before our fathers and God we are always sinners, I told my wife. In the final analysis, my father, too, was preparing me for the same thing, for the same "culture" as the boarding school, and he gave his educational goals probably just as little thought as I did my resisting of them, my disobedience, my failure. While we admittedly didn't understand each other, our cooperation was perfect, I told my wife.

And while I have no idea as to whether or not I loved him, one thing's certain: I often and genuinely felt sorry for him. But still, even when I made him ridiculous occasionally and then felt sorry for him, when, in other words – but always most secretly – I toppled paternal rule, and authority . . . God, then it was not only my father who lost his authority over me, but I, too, lost by becoming frighteningly lonely, I told my wife. I needed a tyrant to reestablish my world order, I told her; my father, however, never tried to replace my toppled order with a new one, such as, for instance, one of our shared vulnerability, or one of truth, I told my wife. In this manner, just as I was a bad boy and a bad student, I was an equally bad Jew, I told my wife. My Jewishness remained a vague circumstance of my birth, just another fault among many, a bald woman in a robe before the mirror, I told my wife. Of course I told her many other things that I no longer remember. I do remember that I totally exhausted her just as I, too, got very tired and am tired even now. Auschwitz, I told my wife, struck me later as simply an elaboration of those virtues in which I have been indoctrinated since childhood. Yes, it all started then, in my childhood, that inexcusable process of breaking my spirit, my incessant urge for survival, I told my wife. I was a modestly eager, not always unobjectionably progressing member of the quiet conspiracy woven against my life. Auschwitz, I told her, appears to me in the image of a father; yes, the two terms, Auschwitz and father, resonate the same echoes in me, I told my wife. And if the observation is that God is an exalted father, then God, too, is revealed to me in the image of Auschwitz, I told my wife. When I finally fell silent and then remained silent for a long time, perhaps even for days after all that talking, my wife appeared to be in pain, tortured, but she didn't seem to have comprehended what I said, or, to be more precise, it seemed as if she failed to understand what I said the way I said it, namely, it seemed as if she didn't notice that I turned against her with all my anger and resentment without any reason (and it was of no use that I was aware of this), for no reason, cruelly, and probably exclusively on the grounds that she listened to me (so as to avoid the use of the word "rebel" here where it doesn't belong). As I said, perhaps my wife assumed that now since I poured forth, threw up, told all this, I would be liberated from it all, as if I could ever be freed from all this. This is, perhaps, what she thought, I wondered, noticing some albeit shy attempts to approach me, to approach me with *understanding*. Naturally, I withdrew from that, naturally I couldn't tolerate any *understanding;* all it would have done would have been to sanctify my vulnerability. But this was nothing compared to that elemental recognition which originated perhaps purely from my *procedure,* from my way of treating my wife or – yes, in the final hours of this radiantly black night I have to use the appropriate word because that alone will purify me – well then, the way I *dispensed* with my wife. Yes. I was this cruel, this intimately cruel to her. It seemed that with this she was once and for all unacceptable in my eyes and to a certain extent – but of course this is an exaggeration – but still, to a certain extent it was as if I murdered her and that she became a witness to it; she observed as I killed a person; and it seemed that this was something for which I could never forgive her. It is superfluous to expound any further on these times, for how long we lived, could live, together in silence after this. I felt deeply depressed, helpless, and deserted, and this time, to such an extent that it couldn't be compensated for, that is to say, it no longer pushed my *work* forward, quite to the contrary, it totally paralyzed it. I am not entirely certain as to whether or not I wasn't secretly expecting help from my wife while internally I was forging accusations, long texts of accusatory speeches – naturally. Be it as it may, I don't believe I gave any visible signs for this.

One day, it was in the evening, if I recall correctly, and actually I am quite certain it was in the evening, and rather late at that, my wife just returned home from somewhere, I didn't know from where, I didn't insist on knowing, I didn't even ask from where;

she was beautiful, and fleetingly, like a rod of lightning from behind thick clouds, I was briefly struck by the thought: "What a beautiful Jewess!" – naturally, shamefully, and sadly, and it seemed that she crossed a greenish blue carpet like traversing the sea, and then, that evening, she, my wife, broke the silence, our silence. It's rather late, my wife said, but she sees that I'm sitting up and reading. She was sorry, she said, but she had some business to attend to but that I wasn't interested in that anyway. That I am sitting there reading, reading or writing, reading *and* writing is all the same, my wife said. Yes, indeed, she said, this has been quite some schooling for her, this whole thing, meaning our marriage. Through me, my wife said, she has come to understand and experience what she didn't and didn't want to understand by her parents' experiences. She didn't because that understanding would simply have killed her as a young girl, she now knows. She said that secretly, in the deep recesses of her soul, she believed herself to be a coward, but now she knows – and she gives significant credit for this to me and the years we spent together – now she knows that that wasn't the case: she simply wanted to live, she had to live. And even now, my wife said, everything within her tells her the same thing: that she wants to live. She pities me, and she is most regretful that she has to pity me feeling so helpless herself. She had tried everything within her power to *save me* (I was quiet, although her choice of words astonished me). She had tried it for nothing else but gratitude, my wife continued, because it was I who showed her the road on which I cannot travel with her, because those wounds are more powerful than my intellect, the wounds which I carry within me and which I could perhaps have overcome, but it seems, or at least it appears so to her, my wife said, that I didn't and still don't want to overcome them, and this has cost us our love, our marriage. Again she said she pitied me, she said they destroyed me but that I indeed remained destroyed, which is something she didn't notice initially; quite to the contrary, my wife said, at first she admired me for the fact that while they destroyed me I was not destroyed. She viewed me that way then, my wife said, but she was wrong. Even that would have been OK, she said, because it didn't evoke any sense of disappointment in her, even though, undoubtedly, she suffered on that account. She repeated that she wanted to save me but that the sterility, futility of all her efforts, her love, and her devotion gradually killed her love, desire, and devotion to me, and left her with nothing but a sense of futility, uselessness, and misery. She said that I often spoke of freedom but that the freedom I so constantly invoked was actually, for me, not the freedom of my profession, my *art* (this is how she put it), in fact I didn't really mean freedom by the word if we understand it to denote space, strength, acceptance, which includes responsibility, yes, love, my wife said. No, my freedom has always been a freedom *from* something or someone, my wife said; it was escape or attack, or both, and without these, it seems, my freedom didn't exist, because apparently it couldn't exist, my wife said. And, thus, if there happened to be no "somethings" or "someones" to escape or attack, then I invented them and created such dependencies, my wife said, so that I had something to escape or attack. And that I had for years now cruelly assigned this awful – she asked to be permitted to be totally frank – this shameful role to her, but not like a lover seeking support from his beloved, not even like a sick man assigning the role to his physician, no, my wife said, I assigned this role to her (to use, again, one of my favorite expressions) like an executioner to his victim. She said I covered her with my spirit, then evoked pity in her, and when I awakened her pity I made her my listener, the listener to my awful childhood and my monstrous stories, and when she wished to become a participant in my stories so that she could lead me out of the labyrinth of these tales, their mud, their quicksand, so that she could lead me to her, to her love, so that afterward we could both, together, walk out of this swamp and leave all behind us like the bad memory of a sickness, then I suddenly let go of her hand (this is how she expressed herself) and began to run away from her back to the swamp. She now no longer has the strength, my wife said, to come after me the second time, and who knows how many times she would need to come after me and lead me out. Because it seems, my wife said, that I have no inclination to come out of there, that there seems to be no way out for me from my awful childhood and monstrous tales, regardless of what she does, even if she gave her life. She knows, she sees, that even that would be done for naught. Yes, when we first chanced upon each other (this is the term my wife used), then it seemed to her as if I wished to teach her how to live, and then she realized to her horror how I was filled with destructive energy and that next to me it was not life but destruction that was to await her. Mine was a sick consciousness, my wife said, a sick and poisoned consciousness (and she repeated it again and again), eternally poisoned and eternally poisoning consciousness, which, my wife said, must be eradicated, must be fled; if one wants to live one must flee from it, she repeated, and she had decided that she wished to live. Here my wife fell silent for a second, and as she stood there with her shoulders a little pulled up, her arms akimbo, lonely, scared, pale, her lipstick smeared, suddenly, or, shall I say, inevitably, the idea occurred to me that, perhaps, she was feeling cold. And then quickly and dryly, like some unpleasant bit of news that will leave its unpleasant taste as soon as she has told it, she added that, yes, there's no point to keeping it secret, she "does have someone," someone whom she was thinking about marrying. And that *he,* she said, was not Jewish. It's rather interesting that I only spoke up at this point, as if from all that my wife had said I found only this kind of information offensive. Who do you think I am?! I screamed at her then, some kind of a perverse race-preserver?! I didn't have to be in Auschwitz, I screamed, to recognize this age and this world and to denounce what I recognized (albeit, admittedly, in a strange way), to deny it in the name of a worldview, understood in a rather practical way, a view which is actually nothing else but the idea of getting along, yes, I screamed, I have no objections, but let's be clear about it, I screamed, let's see it clearly, that what we are talking about is not the assimilation of a race . . . race! – You make me laugh! – to another race – I do have to laugh! – but the individual's total assimilation to present circumstances and existing relationships, I screamed, which circumstances and relationships can be this or that, and it is not worth qualifying their qualities, they are what they are; it is our decision and our *decision* only that is worth, even *essential* to qualify, our decision to complete the total assimilation or our decision not to complete the total assimilation, I screamed, but probably more quietly then. Furthermore, we must, we absolutely must qualify our capabilities as to whether or not we can complete the total assimilation. I have already recognized in my childhood that I was incapable of assimilating myself to the existing, the real, to *life*, and in spite of that, I shouted, I still exist, am real, and live, but in the way I know how. As I had recognized in my early childhood: had I assimilated, it would have killed me even sooner than the fact that I didn't, which will actually kill me anyway. And in that respect it doesn't matter a hill of beans whether I am a Jew or a non-Jew, although being a Jew does undoubtedly have a large advantage here and in this respect – do you understand, I shouted – and only in this respect I am willing to be a Jew; exclusively in this respect do I consider it lucky, particularly lucky, even a blessing not that I am a Jew, for I couldn't care less what I am, but the fact that, labeled a Jew, I was allowed to be in Auschwitz and that on account of my Jewishness I experienced and survived something and faced something; and now I know something once and for all and irrevocably, something that I won't let go of, will never let go of, I shouted. Then I fell silent. Then we divorced. And if I recall my years following this event as years not entirely bleak, that fact is due entirely to my *work*, in those years, as always since then, before then, and, naturally, even during the years of my marriage. I have worked; yes indeed, my work saved me, albeit it saved me for the sake of destruction. In these years I not only made some decisive discoveries but I also recognized then that these recognitions are intricately tied to my fate knot by knot. During those years I also discovered the true nature of my work, which, essentially, is nothing else but digging, continued and continuous digging of the grave others had started for me in the clouds, the wind, in nothingness. In those years I dreamed again of my tasks and hopes based, I know now, on the example of the "Professor." In those years I recognized my life for what it was: as a fact on the one hand and as a spiritual form on the other, or, more precisely, the spiritual form of the survival instinct that no longer can survive, doesn't want to survive, and probably is no longer capable of survival, but one that still and because of it all demands its own, that is to say, its own formation like a rounded glass-hard object so that it could continue to exist, no matter why, no matter for whom – for everyone and no one; for him who is and him who isn't, it doesn't really matter, for those who are ashamed because of us and (perhaps) for us; but which fact as the pure fact of survival I eliminate and put an end to even if and especially if that fact happens to be me.

It happened during those years that I met Dr. Oblath in the forest. In those years I started to take down some notes on my marriage. It was in those years that my wife contacted me again. Once, when, expecting some new prescriptions, I was waiting for her in the usual coffeehouse, she came in leading two children by the hand. A dark-eyed girl with pale dots of scattered freckles around her little nose and a stubborn boy with hard eyes like grayish blue pebbles. "Say hello to the gentleman," she told them. This sobered me up once and for all. Occasionally, like a drab weasel left over after a thorough process of extermination, I run through the city. I listen to a noise, notice an image here or there, as if the smell of occasional memories from the outside set siege to my petrified, sluggish senses. Here and there I stop at a house, a street corner, frightened, with widened nostrils, I look around me horrified, I want to flee but something holds me back. Under my feet the sewer lines roar as if the filthy flow of memories tried to break out of its hidden channels to sweep me away. Let it pass: I am prepared. In my last great effort to pull myself together I have presented my frail and stubborn life – I have presented it so that with the baggage of this life in my raised hands I may go and in the dark stream of the fast-flowing black warmth

I may drown
Lord God
let me drown
forever,
Amen.